A Talent for Murder

A TALENT FOR MURDER

TERESA A. LARUE

FIVE STAR
A part of Gale, Cengage Learning

GALE
CENGAGE Learning·

Farmington Hills, Mich • San Francisco • New York • Waterville, Maine
Meriden, Conn • Mason, Ohio • Chicago

GALE
CENGAGE Learning

LIBRARY OF CONGRESS CATALOGING-IN-PUBLICATION DATA

LaRue, Teresa A.
  A talent for murder / Teresa A. LaRue—First edition.
    pages cm
    ISBN 978-1-4328-3105-9 (hardcover) — ISBN 1-4328-3105-4 (hardcover) — ISBN 978-1-4328-3101-1 (ebook) — ISBN 1-4328-3101-1 (ebook)
    1. Man-woman relationships—Fiction. 2. Murder—Investigation—Fiction. I. Title.
    PS3612.A7755T36 2015
    813'.6—dc23   2015013110

First Edition. First Printing: January 2016
Find us on Facebook– https://www.facebook.com/FiveStarCengage/
Visit our website– http://www.gale.cengage.com/fivestar/
Contact Five Star™ Publishing at FiveStar@cengage.com

Printed in the United States of America
1 2 3 4 5 6 7 20 19 18 17 16

For all those who have shaped my life
My parents, husband, and three wonderful children

ACKNOWLEDGMENTS

Many thanks to Deni Deitz for sifting through her slush pile and giving me this opportunity. And a great big thank you to Alice Duncan for all her patience and help in the editing process.

CHAPTER ONE

Some people seem to attract trouble. My mother, Happy Spencer, is particularly skilled at it. Only when she was involved would a free gardening class lead to murder.

Tonight's class—container water gardening—was scheduled to start in less than twenty minutes. Which meant I'd better get busy hauling all the supplies I'd need for my demonstration outside, or suffer the wrath of my mother.

From the looks of things, Happy had already done more than her share of the work. The potting bench I'd planned to use for my demonstration was already in place, the refreshment table was crammed with enough food to feed the entire town, and six rows of white, wooden chairs were waiting for the arrival of eager students.

As I was dragging out the last terracotta pot, my trouble-loving mother popped up at my side. "Lula Mae's coming tonight," she said. Snatching the pot from my hands, she shuffled to the end of the workbench and heaved it down. It hit the ground with a good, solid thud.

Muttering a quick prayer, I scooted over and scanned the pot for signs of damage. Lucky for her, I didn't find any. Then, as if she thought my ears were stuffed with cotton balls, she repeated her statement about Lula Mae's imminent arrival.

"That's nice," I replied, and set to work arranging the containers in what I thought was an attractive pattern along the front of the workbench. Apparently, my arrangement wasn't up to her standards. She pursed her lips, gave it some thought, then muscled me aside and began to redo the items to suit her own taste.

I held back the retort that threatened to spew out, and turned my attention to sorting out the various plant materials. Before long, she nudged me aside and took over that task, too. An urge to dump over the whole display swept through me. It took every ounce of self-control I could muster to step back and let her do things *her* way.

Unaware of the hurricane building inside me, she went right on talking about Lula Mae's plans. "I suppose that new guy she's dating, Percy something-or-other, will be driving her over. They seem to be joined at the hip these days."

I eyed her warily. "I'm going to bring over the hose now, or would you rather take care of that, too?"

"What, dear?" She tossed me a puzzled look, then gave a little wave and said, "Oh, no. Go right ahead. I'm sure you're quite capable of handling it."

My jaw dropped open in astonishment. Could she really be so oblivious to my feelings?

"The thing is"—she trailed after me as I went to uncoil the hose—"I don't think this guy's any good for her. I mean, there's just something about him that doesn't ring true."

Having been on the receiving end of her interference more than once, I blurted out, "If he makes her happy, then maybe you should just back off. Let them enjoy the moment."

"Makes her happy." Happy snorted. "She's only known the man for what, six weeks? How much can she possibly know about him?" She scrunched up her eyebrows. "Does she know anything about his background? What sort of people he comes from? How much money he has in the bank?"

"I'm sure they'll get around to discussing all that stuff. Besides, it's not like they're planning to run off and get married next week."

She stared at me with that fierce pit-bull look she has. "You mark my words, young lady, nothing good can come from this relationship. I've been around long enough to see my share of trouble, so trust me when I tell you: this relationship is headed for disaster." Her generous, red-painted lips clamped shut, daring me to argue.

For someone so tiny—petite is the word she prefers—my mother is some spitfire when she wants to be. Her flaming red hair may have gotten a little help from a bottle of dye over the years, but her temper hadn't dulled one bit.

"Have you ever thought that maybe you're just . . ." I hesitated a moment, gathered my courage, then spat out the word, "jealous? After all, before he came along Lula Mae depended on you for practically everything."

"Don't be ridiculous!" Her green eyes flashed a warning behind thick, round lenses. "After George died, somebody had to look after her. See that the bills got paid, the legal work taken care of. Lula Mae was certainly in no shape to handle what needed to be done. But, thank goodness, she didn't have to because she's got family, and family—"

"—always stick together," I silently mouthed the words. Deciding not to douse more fuel on the fire, I scooted over to the refreshment table. "Where's that chocolate cake you promised to bake?"

Though her nose was still a trifle out of joint, she grudgingly replied, "If you'll open your eyes, you'll see it. It's right there next to the cold drinks."

I located the cake with ease, a three-story affair with thick, rich frosting. It was right where she'd said it would be, along with a wide assortment of other culinary delights: apple pie, deviled eggs, fried chicken with mashed potatoes and gravy. Did I mention that Happy happens to be one of the best cooks this side of the Mississippi?

When she'd come up with this idea of offering free gardening classes, I'd argued there was no need to serve a meal. Maybe have coffee, a few cookies, nothing elaborate. "Nonsense," she'd said, "I'm not inviting friends and neighbors to our place without offering them more than a few measly crumbs."

Though I'd quickly pointed out that this wasn't her home, but a place of business, in the end it didn't matter. Happy had already started planning the menu. So, here we were—the table stuffed with all sorts of scrumptious food—waiting for the arrival of eager students.

Hoping to get back on her good side, I trotted over and gave her a hug. "No wonder I haven't seen you all day."

She pushed me away. "Don't think you can fool me, young lady. I know exactly what you're up to, and you're not getting back into my good graces that easily." Though her words sounded gruff, I could tell she was pleased by the well-deserved praise.

A few minutes before six, I scooted out to the front gate and staked out the parking lot. What if no one showed up? What if all this . . . effort . . . was for nothing? I was well on my way to becoming a frazzled mess when a police car came barreling into the parking lot.

That got my attention. I stopped worrying about how many students we'd have at tonight's class and got busy worrying about other things. Like: had I broken any laws? I couldn't think of any. Well, maybe I hadn't come to a complete stop outside the library yesterday, but how would the police know that?

My first instinct was to hide. But it was too late for that. Lieutenant Griggs had already spotted me. There was nothing I could do but stand my ground. And I did. I even had the audacity to admire how well he filled out that crisp, blue uniform he wore as he climbed out of his cruiser.

With a quick nod in my direction, he hustled around the vehicle and opened the passenger door. Mrs. Cobb, preacher's wife and former school librarian, emerged in a bright yellow dress. Her fluffy mass of short, blonde hair glistened in the sunlight. "Thank you so much, Steven," she said, in that soft melodious voice I knew so well. "I don't know what I would have done if you hadn't come along."

He smiled politely. "It was my pleasure, ma'am."

"Oh, Kate," Mrs. Cobb said when she caught sight of me, "my car broke down a couple of miles down the road. Steven here drove by and offered me a lift." She beamed a smile in his direction. "What a fine young man he's turned into. Of course, I had serious doubts about his future when he was going through those awkward teen years. Especially after he started hanging out with that trouble-maker, Brad Johnson."

"Last I heard Brad is some big-wig at a PR firm in Los Angeles," Steven told her.

"Well," she said, giving a weak smile, "at least he managed to put that lying ability to good use."

Shifting the conversation to safer ground, I said, "If you need a tow truck, I can run into the office and call somebody." By sheer willpower, I kept my attention focused on Mrs. Cobb and not on the man standing beside her.

"That won't be necessary," he said, forcing me to acknowledge his presence. "I've already radioed Jim. He's on his way."

"That's right, dear. Steven has taken care of everything." Oblivious to my growing discomfort, she went on, "I'm so excited about tonight's class." Her clear, blue eyes glistened. "I've been searching for a new project to tackle. When Happy told me about her idea, it sounded so interesting, I couldn't wait to get started."

Finally, she seemed to sense my unease. Leaning over, she

patted my shoulder. "There's no need to fret, dear. I've taken it upon myself to let some of the girls at church know about the class. I'm sure the place will be filled with students." She tossed a smile at Steven. "Perhaps we can even talk this fine, young man into attending."

I was already nervous about speaking before a crowd. I didn't need to see Steven's face in the audience. "I'm sure he has better things to do."

Steven turned to Mrs. Cobb. "What did you say this class was about?"

"Nothing that you'd find interesting," I said.

Storm-gray eyes shifted in my direction. "I've been thinking about getting a new hobby. This gardening stuff might be just the thing I'm looking for."

"Try fishing," I said. "It's a lot more manly."

"Seems to me digging holes in the ground is pretty manly work."

Mrs. Cobb shot me a sly look. "I don't mean to change the subject, dear, but didn't you tell me that you'd broken up with that fellow from up north? I believe he sold real estate."

"He sold insurance," I said. "And that was over ages ago."

She let out a whoosh of air. "I'm sure that was a relief to your poor mama. She was mighty worried about you for a while there."

Now she had my dander up. "It was none of my mama's business."

"I'm sure Steven would agree with me." Mrs. Cobb looked to him for support. "That man was all wrong for you. Why, he probably would have dragged you off to one of those big cities up north, where no one knows their neighbor and crime is rampant. Then your poor mama would have been stuck here, all alone, having to fend for herself."

Taking his cue from her, Steven said, "Shame on you, Katherine Renee Spencer. How could you even think of doing such a cruel thing to your *poor* mama?"

I shot him a dirty look. He knew as well as I did, how capable my *poor* mama was. "Don't you have some place to be?"

He couldn't hold back a grin. "Now that you mention it, I should be getting back to the station." He gave Mrs. Cobb a wink. "Be sure and let me know when the next class meets. I might decide to join you."

"It would be our pleasure," Mrs. Cobb said, looking entirely too satisfied with herself.

We both stood there admiring the scenery as Steven sauntered back to his cruiser. No doubt about it: he was one fine specimen. Not that I was interested. Not in the least.

"I'm not very fond of the girl that boy's seeing now," Mrs. Cobb said. "Thinks she owns the town just because her daddy has all that money."

I cleared my throat. "I heard they were getting married."

She shook her head. "If I'm any judge of character, that relationship won't last. He'll come to his senses before long, get his life back on track, and marry some sensible girl. One who'll appreciate what a fine man he is."

An unladylike snort popped out. "Just like I got my life back on track by dumping the guy from up north?"

She smiled smugly. "Exactly."

Hoping to crush any matchmaking ideas she had, I said, "Well, I'm not in the market for a boyfriend at the moment. My work keeps me busy. And when I'm not working, I—"

"That's interesting, dear," she broke in, dismissing me as if I were nothing more than a pesky gnat. "If you'll excuse me, I'd better find a seat." Then she breezed through the freshly painted gate, and called to one of her friends.

CHAPTER TWO

I would've gone after Mrs. Cobb, but a carload of students spilled into the parking lot. Slapping on a smile, I ran over to join Happy in greeting them.

The first group was made up of members of the local garden club. Then came a couple of young mothers pushing strollers, a few old friends, four or five of our best customers, what must've been Mrs. Cobb's entire flock of Sunday school teachers, and finally one unexpected surprise—Camilla Davenport.

Don't get me wrong. Camilla is one of our best customers. Only it's her gardener, Henry, who does all the buying, planting, fertilizing, and pretty much anything else that involves the slightest contact with that ugly four letter word—d i r t. She probably doesn't even know she is one of our best customers.

I darted a look around, hoping Happy hadn't spotted Camilla. Good. At the moment she was reigning over a display of azaleas as she chatted with a short, bald man in baggy, brown pants. My attention shifted back to Camilla. There was something here that didn't add up. Why would a reasonably sane woman show up in a place where she knew she wouldn't be welcomed?

Even the way she was dressed made her stand out. While everyone else had donned shorts or slacks for the occasion, she had on a tailored, navy suit that was probably worth more than my entire wardrobe. Her short, silver hair was carefully styled, and even her makeup looked expertly applied. All this, for a

16

gardening class.

My instincts shrieked—no way.

I moseyed down the aisle in her direction. "Camilla." I strove for a light tone. "How nice to see you again. I never realized you were that interested in plants."

Two vertical slashes popped up between wide-spaced hazel eyes. "I'm always interested in learning new skills." Her bony chin tilted upward in defiance.

Not wanting to offend one of our best customers, I quickly backpedaled. "Of course you are." I scanned the area. "I don't see Henry anywhere. Will he be attending tonight's class?"

"Why on earth would my gardener attend a social function with me?"

Social function. Hmm, so that was what this was.

I shrugged. "No reason, I guess." Except he's the one who's going to get stuck taking care of any plants you buy, I wanted to shout. "I just thought—"

"What? That I don't have a brain in my head. That I'm not perfectly capable of learning some simple, little task like"—she flapped a well-manicured hand in the air—"sticking a bunch of plants into a pot."

"I'm afraid there's a little more to it than that," I began, then noting her fierce scowl, changed course, "but I'm sure you have lots of artistic ability. Everyone in town talks about what a showplace your yard is." Thanks to that wonderful gardener of yours, I longed to add.

For the moment, she seemed appeased. I began to scoot past her, but something made me turn back. "You do realize that Lula Mae will be here tonight?"

Her eyes narrowed. "I assumed she would be."

What was going on here? You would be hard put to find anyone in town who didn't know about the long-standing feud between the two women. It had started back in their high school days when both women—girls, I should say—had fallen in love with the same man. The man, I'm proud to say, who later became my Uncle George. Though Camilla had gone on to marry a well-to-do businessman, she had never quite forgiven Lula Mae for stealing her first love.

"I just thought you might not want to—" I began.

"Is it true what I heard," she broke in, "that she's dating that new man in town? I believe someone said his name is Percy Moss."

Something about the way she lingered over his name aroused my suspicions. "That's right. As a matter of fact"—I glanced at my watch—"I'm surprised they aren't here by now."

"You think this . . . thing . . . between them is serious?"

"Who knows?" I said, squirming about under her intense gaze.

"I've heard the man is already involved in a serious relation-ship."

Warning bells went off in my head. "Who told you that?"

"I realize that . . . George"—she stumbled over his name—"hasn't been gone all that long. Perhaps Lula Mae and your mother should book a trip. Go somewhere bright and sunny to take her mind off her loss."

The warning bells began to clang louder. "Who did you say Percy was seeing?"

"Uh . . ." Camilla suddenly looked flustered, "I really need to speak to Florence Cobb about the senior citizens' potluck," she said, then bolted away like some spooked animal.

I stood there a moment contemplating the matter, then forced myself to move on. As I mingled with the noisy crowd, I caught sight of my mother standing alone near the end of the workbench. She motioned me over.

Feeling like a lamb on its way to the slaughterhouse, I excused myself and headed in her direction. Out of the corner of my eye

I caught sight of Lucille Crandell standing by the gate wearing a big, floppy straw hat and a pair of enormous, white sunglasses. I waved, but she stood there scanning the crowd, acting as if she didn't see me.

"What's that woman doing here?" Happy demanded, glaring at me as if I'd committed some crime.

"What woman?" I tried to feign ignorance. "Lucille? Mrs. Cobb?"

"Don't play dumb with me, young lady. You know perfectly well 'what woman.' "

That narrowed the field considerably. "I guess she happens to be interested in plants."

Her pit-bull demeanor returned. "She has no business being here."

"Last time I heard, this was still a free country."

"Don't you lecture me, young lady." She started across the courtyard.

Before she could get far, I reached out and snagged her arm. "If you go over there and cause a scene, you're liable to scare away all our other students." And be the subject of tonight's dinner conversations.

"I suppose you're right." She knew the condition of our checkbook as well as I did. "She can stay, but I'm going to be keeping my eye on her." Her words picked up momentum. "Yes siree. She'd better watch her step because—"

"While you're busy keeping an eye on her," I said, "why don't you go say hello to Lucille. See if she plans on attending tonight's class."

"Lucille." Happy's eyes brightened. "Where'd you see her?"

I gestured toward the entrance. "She was standing next to the gate a minute ago." I scanned the area. "That's strange. I know she was here. She had on one of those floppy, straw hats like you always wear when you're working in the vegetable garden."

"Are you feeling all right?" Happy frowned, then reached up and felt my forehead. "Maybe you'd better go inside and rest. I can—"

"I'm fine." I jerked away. "You just go do—whatever it is you need to do—and let me get started with my lesson plans."

She cast me a skeptical glance, then marched away, leaving me to fumble through my presentation alone.

I scooted over to the workbench and dug out my notes. I waited a moment for everyone to get settled. "As most of you know, tonight we'll be discussing how to set up a water garden using various types of containers. First, we'll take a look at what kinds of containers are appropriate for our use, then we'll move on to the different plant materials available, and finish up with a few tips on maintenance."

Most of the audience seemed interested in what I had to say, with one exception: Camilla Davenport. Her sharp, hazel eyes were constantly on the move. No doubt watching for the happy couple to arrive.

CHAPTER THREE

Near the end of my demonstration, Lula Mae and Percy finally sauntered in. Holding hands, they made their way down the center aisle, settling into two empty seats along the front.

Camilla's eyes held such venom that I lost my train of thought and had to backtrack. "As I was saying, some of the hardier water lilies can stay outdoors as long as their roots don't freeze." After a short question-and-answer session, I wrapped things up.

Happy quickly shuffled forward and announced that refreshments would be served. Eager students popped out of their seats and trotted after her. I began to wonder how many had actually come for the food and regarded the class as a necessary inconvenience.

Realizing how rapidly the sun was dipping toward the horizon, I ducked inside the office and flipped on the fake gaslights we'd installed a couple of years ago. At the time, Happy had complained about their cost, but I thought they were well worth the money we'd spent. They added an old-world charm to our place that made it stand out from some of those newer garden centers which had recently sprung up along the highway. Even when customers couldn't remember the name of our place—The Flower Patch—they always seemed to remember it was "that place with all the lights."

"Yoo-hoo, Kate." Lula Mae's screechy voice called out to me as I stepped out of the office. She charged toward me, dragging a reluctant Percy in her wake.

I didn't get it. What could she possibly see in this man? He was short and pudgy, looked at the world through washed-out blue eyes, and had a mass of dingy white hair that cried out for a good bleach job.

Okay, so maybe I wasn't being entirely fair. There was probably no man on earth who could ever measure up to my Uncle George. It was just that this man was so small. And Uncle George had been so . . . big. He'd had big hands, big bones, big features, but more importantly, he'd had the biggest heart of anyone I'd ever known.

Evidently, however, there had to be something about this colorless man that was worthwhile, because Lula Mae's dark brown eyes practically glowed. And that pale white skin of hers had a hint of color to it that I hadn't seen in years.

"We wanted you to be the first to know," she said, "Percy and I are getting married." She shoved her age-spotted hand into my face to display the fat diamond sparkling on her finger.

I felt as if someone had punched me in the stomach. "When did this happen?"

"About an hour ago." She grinned. "That's how come we were so late getting here." From her three-inch height advantage—two inches of actual flesh and bone, and another inch of heel—she gazed lovingly down on Percy.

I must have scrunched up my face, or made some other gesture that betrayed my true feelings about the matter, because Percy suddenly snapped to attention. He drew himself up stiffly and took over the story. "That's right. A mere two hours," he glanced at his watch, "and fifteen minutes ago, I took this lovely aunt of yours out for dinner and asked her to become my wife. Bringing me great joy, she accepted. We hope you"—his gaze traveled over to include Happy, who was busy serving refreshments, blissfully unaware of her sister's impending marriage—"and your mother, of course, will do us the honor of attending the ceremony."

I had a pretty good idea what Happy's reply to his invitation was going to be, and I can't say I wanted to be around when she shared it with him. "Sure. I'd . . . that is . . . we'd love to come." I reached over, gave Lula Mae's broad shoulders a squeeze, then made some sappy remark about how lucky they were to have found each other.

Lula Mae beamed.

"So, when is this big event going to take place?" I hoped to hear an answer like: a year from now. Or, better yet: two years from now.

"Oh, we don't intend to waste a moment, do we, honey-pie?" Lula Mae's adoring, gaze locked onto Percy. "At our age we simply can't afford the luxury of waiting. After all, who knows what tomorrow may bring?"

I started to feel a little nauseated. Okay, truth be told, a whole lot nauseated. But who could blame me? My aunt . . . engaged . . . to this man. Uncle George was probably turning over in his grave at this very moment.

Slipping an arm around Lula Mae's ample waist, Percy said, "Your aunt is right. We plan to tie the old knot as quickly as possible. Nothing fancy. Just a small, family affair. In fact, we could hold the ceremony near that little gazebo in your mother's backyard." He glanced at Lula Mae. "What do you think, honey-cakes?"

"I think that's a wonderful idea," she said, as if he were some kind of genius. "Don't you agree, Kate?"

"Okay by me." I wasn't the one she had to worry about.

As if she could read my thoughts, Lula Mae's expression dimmed. "I suppose we should go over and break the news to Happy." She didn't sound all that pleased by the prospect.

"Maybe you should wait until everyone leaves," I said, hoping to postpone the explosion that was certain to follow her revelation. "That way she'll have time to join you in celebrating the good news."

"I did promise your mama that I'd help her with the refreshments." She sounded relieved. "Do me a favor. Keep your uncle-to-be company while I run over and give her a hand." She shot Percy an apologetic smile, then slipped the enormous ring off her finger and tucked it away in her purse. "It won't be there for long," she promised. "Just until we get a chance to break the news to Happy."

A look of displeasure crossed his face. Then his eyes glazed over, and it was hard to tell what he was thinking. All those questions Happy had thrown at me earlier came to mind. Now was my chance to get some answers. I began with the obvious. "Where are you from, Mr. Moss?"

A smile came easily to his lips. Too easily, if you asked me. "Call me Percy, or Uncle Percy, if you like."

"Okay . . . Percy." I had enough trouble spitting out his given name without the uncle part tacked on. "What part of the country are you from?"

"Nowhere in particular." He pulled a set of keys from his pocket and used the end of one to clean his nails. "In my line of work I do a good bit of traveling."

I latched on to that piece of information. "What kind of work would that be?"

"Oh, a little of this and a little of that," he replied, still digging at his nails.

I studied him closely. Was he one of those intensely private people who resent questions of any kind, or was there some other reason he seemed so reluctant to discuss his personal life?

As if sensing my suspicions, he glanced up. "I'm in sales." He pocketed the keys. "Pharmaceuticals, mostly."

"Here in the southeast," I asked, hoping to pry more information from him, "or up north?"

24

The keys came back out of his pocket. "Outside Atlanta, mostly."

"I guess you must make pretty good money, considering how many people are on meds these days."

He shrugged. "I do all right."

I moved on to the next question. "I haven't noticed you at church. You are a church-going man, aren't you?"

His gaze shifted to where Lula Mae was pouring drinks. "I've been visiting various churches around town." He cleared his throat. "I probably just haven't visited yours yet."

"Lula Mae is a member of my church," I pointed out.

"Yes, well . . . we haven't exactly had time to discuss the matter." He shrugged. "Everything has been happening so fast."

That was an understatement. Uncle George had been dead less than six months. Now here Lula Mae was getting married again. It was hard to wrap my mind around the idea.

Before I could voice my opinion concerning the matter, Mrs. Cobb bore down on us with a determined look on her face. "Kate, I'm so glad I caught you. I need a little advice about a matter."

Out of the corner of my eye, I noticed Percy's shoulders sag in relief. My gut told me Happy was right—there was definitely something wrong about this man.

"I meant to ask you earlier," Mrs. Cobb went on, drawing my attention away from Percy, "I have some ladies coming by for brunch tomorrow and the rose bushes around my patio are covered with the most horrible black spots. I'm ashamed for anyone to see them. Of course, I realize I can't get rid of the spots overnight, but I do want to assure the ladies that I have things under control." Tirade finished, Mrs. Cobb's gaze shifted in Percy's direction.

I made the introductions, skipping the part about his recent engagement.

Mrs. Cobb held out her hand. "I don't think I've seen you around town, Mr. Moss. Are you new to the area?"

"I haven't been in town all that long." He reached for her hand. "Perhaps you could suggest some good restaurants."

She thought about it a minute. "Well, there's Bessie's Kitchen if you like barbecue."

"Love it," he replied, still hanging on to her hand.

"If you're looking for something more upscale, there's the Harbor Lights."

"Sounds perfect."

I decided it was time to put a damper on Percy's interest. "Mrs. Cobb's husband is the preacher down at Community Fellowship Church." Through narrowed eyes, I added, "The church Lula Mae attends."

Percy snatched his hand back. "It's really hot out here. I think I'll go get something to drink. If you ladies will excuse me." He gave a quick nod, then lit out toward the refreshment table as if a hive of bees was chasing him down.

"What a strange man," Mrs. Cobb said as she watched him flee.

You don't know how strange, I thought, before launching into an explanation of her black spot problem and the recommended cure.

It seemed those awful black spots weren't Mrs. Cobb's only problem. By the time I made my escape, Percy had long since vanished. I guess it was just as well. I needed time to get used to the idea of Lula Mae being engaged.

Like that was possible.

CHAPTER FOUR

Everything seemed to be humming along nicely, until I spotted Camilla headed toward the refreshment table. In five seconds flat, I scrambled across the stretch of ground that separated us and clamped a hand on her arm. "Why don't you find a seat somewhere, and I'll bring you a plate of food."

"Don't be silly." She wrestled her arm from my grasp. "I'm perfectly capable of fixing my own plate. Besides, I have a few things I want to discuss with your aunt."

I glanced over my shoulder and spotted Lula Mae at the buffet table. "She's a little busy at the moment. Why don't you tell me what's on your mind and I'll make sure she gets the message."

Dismissing my offer, Camilla plowed across the courtyard toward Lula Mae. Happy saw her coming and tried to cut her off. "Well, if it isn't the first lady of Port Springs," she said, slipping into her banty rooster mode. "What can I do for you?"

"How about the satisfaction of packing your bags and moving across the country," Camilla said with a smirk.

"Afraid I can't do that. My daughter and I have a business to run. But seems to me you have nothing holding you here. Maybe you should pack up your bags and move across the country. Settle somewhere more suited to your temperament, like the middle of the desert with the rest of the snakes and scorpions."

Camilla crossed her arms and glared down at Happy. "Very funny."

Happy grinned like someone who had just won the lottery. "I thought so."

Before this verbal bantering could escalate into an all out war, I snatched a plate off the table and said, "Camilla, what can I get you to eat? A piece of fried chicken? Some mashed potatoes and gravy?" Without waiting for a reply, I began to slap food onto the plate.

She wrinkled her nose in disgust. "I never eat fried food." Elbowing Happy aside, she strode toward the end of the table where Lula Mae was busy handing out glasses of iced tea. Seeing her old nemesis standing there, Lula Mae's eyes widened in alarm.

Camilla dug into the suitcase she called a purse and pulled out a business card. "Here," she said, thrusting it toward Lula Mae.

Lula Mae snatched the card out of her hand and held it out at arm's length. "Lillian's Travel Agency," she read aloud, then glanced up in confusion.

"Now that your husband's passed on," Camilla explained, "I thought a change of scenery might do you some good. It certainly helped me when my Theodore passed away."

Happy and I exchanged looks. Camilla, concerned about Lula Mae's welfare? My instincts screamed: no way.

Always the big sister, Happy scooted over and plucked the card from Lula Mae's hand. "I don't think Lula Mae's going to be needing any change of scenery. She has family to help her through this difficult time."

Lula Mae jerked the card out of Happy's hands. "I don't know, a trip might be just the thing I need to get my mind off things. Of course, I'll have to check with—"

Realizing where she was headed, I stepped to Lula Mae's side. "Lula Mae has too much to do right now to be taking any trips."

Camilla's gaze locked with mine. "At a time like this, your aunt needs a distraction from her troubles. Something to occupy her time. I find a trip refreshes the mind, as well as the body."

Lula Mae's eyes narrowed. "What's this sudden concern with my health about? You and I have never exactly been friends. Not since you tried to steal George away from me."

"I tried to steal George from you?" Camilla was almost shouting. "George and I were a couple until you came along and ruined everything. I'd already started planning my wedding. Had my bridesmaids lined up, had already started looking at dresses."

Lula Mae's upper body puffed out like a bull ready to charge. "George told me he never had any intention of marrying you. He only went out with you two times. After that, you wouldn't leave him alone. He said you kept following him around, calling him, bringing over plates of food." She stuck her chin up in the air. "I think people who do things like that are called stalkers nowadays."

"Why, you old biddy!" Camilla's face contorted in fury. She glanced around, then snatched up a bucket of ice and hurled its contents at Lula Mae.

As cold pellets slammed into Lula Mae's well-rounded frame, she sucked in a breath, then let out an ear-piercing squeal. Her gaze swept over the area, settled on a pitcher of tea. She grabbed it, then hurled the sweet liquid right into Camilla's face. "Take that, you nasty cow!"

All around people stopped to stare at the feuding pair. Before Camilla could retaliate, I stepped between them. "That's enough drama for one day, ladies." I glanced over at Happy. "Why don't you take Lula Mae back to the house, while I find a couple of towels so Camilla can dry off."

As Happy hustled Lula Mae away, Mrs. Cobb, always eager

to be of service, hurried over. She located a couple of kitchen towels and handed them to Camilla. "I haven't seen you around much lately," she said as Camilla dried off. "What have you been doing with yourself?"

Camilla's body went rigid. "Uh, I have lots of projects going at the moment. Most days, I don't have time to sit down and eat a decent meal." She glanced at her watch. "Oops, look at the time. I've really got to be going." Then, before Mrs. Cobb tried to wrangle her into one of her endless charity projects, she hightailed it out of there.

I, on the other hand, wasn't so lucky. I got talked into potting up a few dozen houseplants to cheer up the residents at the old folks' home. Not that I'm against cheering up old folks. It's just that with Happy and Lula Mae around, I figure I did more than my share already.

A few minutes later, Happy and Lula Mae returned. Handing the refreshment table into their capable hands, I decided to take a well-deserved break. Ambling away from the crowd, I plopped down on one of the benches we'd tucked around the place for non-gardening spouses and slipped off my shoes.

I was sitting there, enjoying the warm night air, when I heard the sound of muffled voices in the greenhouse off to my left. Which was strange, considering there weren't any lights on, and none of our students had any business being in there. Tucking my shoes back on, I crept over to investigate.

"Did you see what that woman did to me?" The voice belonged to Camilla; I was sure of it. But how could that be? I saw her headed toward the parking lot ten minutes ago.

"And what was all that smooching and hand holding about?" she went on. "You promised me you weren't going to see that old biddy anymore."

"Take it easy, my dear," came Percy's smooth reply. "You don't want your blood pressure to go through the roof. Besides, there's nothing to worry about. I can explain everything."

"I'm listening." Her tone implied that his explanation had better be good.

"Look, can't we discuss this later? Say, tomorrow night over dinner? You could give Pricilla the night off so we can be alone."

There was a pause. "What about that woman?"

"Aw, honey cakes. She means nothing to me. You know that. How could I even think about looking at another woman as long as I have you?"

"Seems to me, you were doing a whole lot more than looking when you came in."

"That was just business," he said. "I have to pretend to be interested in her. Like I told you: I'm putting together this business deal, and I'm hoping she'll invest a big chunk of that money her husband left her."

Her tone softened. "I told you I would be happy to give you the money. Theodore left me well off. How much do you need?"

"I appreciate your willingness to help," he said. "But I don't want you, or anyone else—especially those kids of yours—to think I'm just after your money."

"Oh, Percy. It doesn't matter what they think. I want to help you. With your business sense and my money, we'll own this town."

There was a moment of silence, then Percy said, "You can't imagine how much that means to me. To know you have that much faith in me. I'm . . . I'm simply overwhelmed."

"Then you'll take my money?"

There was another moment of silence. "If you insist."

"Good," she replied. "Now go tell that woman you won't be needing her money. And make it clear to her that you and I are together."

"I'll do it immediately," he promised.

"You can come by tomorrow night, around seven. I'll have

Pricilla prepare some of that chicken Kiev you love so much before she takes off."

"You're terrific," Percy said. "You know that, don't you?"

Camilla cleared her throat. "Yes, well, don't forget it."

There was a brief interval of silence, which I refused to speculate about, then I heard footsteps clopping toward the door. Not wanting to be caught snooping, I slithered into the shadow of the building and tried not to breathe too loudly. Moments later, Camilla slipped through the door and tore off down the pathway, headed for the parking lot.

A few seconds later, Percy emerged, wearing a smug smile. Unlike Camilla, he seemed to be in no hurry. He took the time to straighten his tie, smooth back his hair, and button his jacket, before sauntering toward the refreshment table.

My adrenaline kicked into gear. Stalking after him, I watched as he stacked his plate with an assortment of goodies, all the while chatting with Lula Mae as if he hadn't just been double-timing her with her lifelong enemy.

He even managed to do the impossible—he got a smile out of Happy.

It was all I could do not to run over there and yell, "Impostor. Liar." But I realized it wouldn't do any good. Lula Mae was too far gone to listen to reason.

CHAPTER FIVE

The next morning it seemed as if Happy's idea of offering free gardening classes might pay off. Our first customer of the day turned out to be the scrawny brunette who belonged to the local gardening club. She strolled up and down the aisles, pausing now and then to read a label. Brimming with enthusiasm, Happy grabbed a wagon (yes, one of those shiny red things that kids haul around) and darted over to offer her services.

Stifling a yawn, I trotted inside the main building and put on a pot of coffee. While it percolated, I puttered about straightening the tool and seed display. It wasn't long until I heard a car turn into the parking lot. I peeked out the window in time to see a white Mercedes roll to a stop. A tall, black man burst from the car and rushed around to open the rear door.

Though the temperature must have been hovering somewhere in the high seventies, Camilla Davenport emerged, dressed in a white, long-sleeved blouse and beige slacks. A bright yellow scarf was wrapped around her head, turban style.

There was no need to rush out and offer help because she marched right into the office as if she owned the place. "Katherine, thank goodness you're not busy. I have a guest coming by this evening, and I simply must have a few plants to brighten up the place."

I absolutely, positively, hate being called Katherine. No one calls me that—not even my mother. Furthermore, I resented her implication that I wasn't busy. After all, someone had to make the coffee. But a quick glance at the stack of bills on my desk made me grit my teeth and, through sheer force of will, pleasantly ask, "Just what did you have in mind?"

She batted a well-manicured hand in the air, setting the numerous stones on her fingers flashing and the jumble of bracelets around her wrists jangling. "It doesn't really matter. You're the expert. Whatever you think is best. The problem is: I'm in a bit of a hurry. I have an appointment with Pierre to have my hair done. And he hates to be kept waiting. Why don't you pick out five or six plants and Thomas will help you load them."

Several months ago, we began potting up a variety of houseplants in attractive containers for people in search of a quick gift—another one of my mother's creative ideas. Considering how many of her friends, or their various relatives, ended up in the hospital, the idea had netted us a tidy wad of cash.

With dollar signs dancing in my head, I steered her toward the greenhouse, the sight of last night's rendezvous. As we entered the building, I studied her face, looking for signs of guilt, but there was nothing there to betray her. After taking a quick look around, she said, "I'll take them."

"Which ones?" I asked.

"All of them."

"All of them," I managed to splutter out the words, knowing there must be at least fifteen plants on display.

She gave me a puzzled look.

Before she could change her mind, I whipped out my calculator and quoted her a figure. She didn't even bat an eyelash at the amount. "By the way, I want to apologize for my behavior last night." She dug out her checkbook. "I had no business ruining your little class. I'm sure you put a lot of thought and effort into your presentation." She smiled. "I hope this purchase makes up for some of the embarrassment I caused you."

So that was the reason behind this sudden need for greenery. "Don't give it another thought."

She concentrated on filling out the check, then tore it off and handed it to me. "You will extend my apologies to your aunt and mother, I hope."

"Sure." Once I had the check safely tucked away in my shirt pocket, I decided to do a little probing. "Looks like you're planning on throwing a party."

Her face lit up. "No party, just a little celebration with the special man in my life."

A feeling of dread settled over me. "Percy Moss wouldn't happen to be your dinner guest tonight, would he?"

"What if he is?" Her chin jutted out in defiance. "It's not as if he's spoken for."

A surge of anger swept through me. "I'd say he's about as close to the altar as you can get without actually being there."

The creases between her brows deepened. "What's that suppose to mean?"

"It means, while Percy has been getting cozy with you, he's gotten himself engaged to Lula Mae."

Her hazel eyes narrowed. "That's impossible."

"Not only is it possible," I said, "but the wedding's supposed to take place within the next couple of weeks."

"I don't know where you got such a foolish notion from, but—"

"I got the 'foolish notion,' as you put it, from the happy couple themselves. Last night. Right after the gardening class."

Her lips clamped together so tightly, they nearly disappeared.

Wondering if I'd gone too far, I slapped my hand over my shirt pocket in case she wanted her check back. But money seemed to be the last thing on her mind. She made some comment about killing that double-crossing scoundrel, then whirled around and stomped out the door.

My ears were still ringing from the sound of the car door slamming when Thomas bustled inside to help me haul the sea of greenery to the car. We stuffed what we could into the trunk; the rest, he promised to come back for. Then, with a wave of his hand, he was off, sending white shells spewing in all directions.

As soon as Happy finished helping the scrawny brunette, she came barreling over. By that time, I was busy with my watering chores. "What in heaven's name did Camilla want with all those plants? Everybody in town knows she ain't the least bit interested in anything green—unless it's money, of course." She paused to chuckle at her own witticism.

I flicked off the nozzle and began to roll up the hose. "Who knows? Maybe she's looking for a new hobby."

Happy snorted. "More than likely, she's got a man tucked away somewhere. One that's into plants."

"I'm not sure how 'into plants' her dinner guest is, but—"

"Why, that old faker," Happy said, "I bet she's gonna scatter all those plants around so she can pretend she has a green thumb. Wait till I tell Lula Mae. She'll get a real kick out of it."

"I don't think that's such a good idea," I said, perhaps a little too quickly.

Squeezing her face into one of those mother looks that's designed to wheedle a confession out of the strongest of offspring, she asked, "And why not?"

I held out as long as I could. Honestly. "Because her dinner guest happens to be none other than Percy Moss," I finally said, annoyed at myself for giving in.

Her voice rose by several decibels. "Lula Mae's Percy Moss?"

"Is there another man around here with that name?"

"Why, that woman is nothing but a low down, double-digging weasel."

"You're calling her a weasel. What about him? He's the one engaged to one woman while sneaking around with another."

"What do you mean—engaged?" She fairly spat the word out.

I scooted around a table of herbs before answering. "Didn't Lula Mae and Percy tell you?"

Her eyes narrowed. "Tell me what?"

For safety reasons, I decided to put a little more distance between us, moving two tables over to the mint section. "That she and Percy are getting married."

"What!" Fury contorted her features. "How did—when did—?" She took a deep breath, and tried to get hold of her temper.

"It happened last night. Just before class. They were planning on telling you after everyone left."

"What on earth is wrong with that crazy sister of mine? How can she even consider marrying that louse?"

"Maybe she's lonely."

I was rewarded with a scathing look. "She has family to keep her company."

"Maybe he does nice things for her. Like driving her where she needs to go."

"She doesn't need him for that. I took her to the grocery store last Friday."

"Well . . ." My mind raced to come up with another reasonable explanation. "Maybe he listens to all her problems."

Happy folded her arms across her chest. "And I don't?"

I was running out of ideas. "I don't know. Maybe he's brainwashed her. How should I know why she's marrying the louse?"

In a fleeting second Happy's expression went from one of pure fury to one of despair. "How on earth are we going to break the news to her?"

"Who says we have to break the news to her? She'll figure it out soon enough."

She shook her head. "It wouldn't be right. We can't let her go running around town making a fool of herself." She cast a hopeful look in my direction. "Someone has to tell her. Someone who cares about her. Someone who can break the news to her gently."

"There's no way you're dragging me into this mess," I said, folding my arms across my chest. "She's your sister—you tell her."

"But I know she'd take it so much better coming from you. Being her favorite niece and all."

"As you very well know," I said, not falling for her ploy, "I'm her only niece. And the answer is still no."

She chewed on her thoughts a moment. "You're right. Maybe we shouldn't tell her. This dinner could just be a business meeting." She began to warm to the idea. "Yeah, that's probably all it is. Some kind of business meeting."

I stared at her in disbelief. "Yeah, right. And the tooth fairy's real."

"Oh, all right," she gave in. "I'll tell her. But don't go blaming me if she has a nervous breakdown and winds up in the loony ward." Having said her piece, she stomped off ranting about how young people have no respect for their elders these days.

CHAPTER SIX

I can't say I was too surprised when Lula Mae turned up at our supper table that evening. I even felt a tad guilty for guzzling down a huge plate of food while she only picked at hers. But who could resist the taste of fresh corn, butter beans, fried chicken, and cornbread muffins slathered with gobs of butter? It was definitely not a night for counting fat grams.

I did pause from stuffing my face long enough to notice the fat diamond she'd worn so proudly the night before was missing from her finger.

"I just don't understand," Lula Mae said for about the hundredth time. "Why did this have to happen? Everything was going so well. Now everyone in town will know how foolish I've been."

"Don't worry about it," Happy said. "You'll get through this the same way you've lived through every other crisis in your life—with the help of your family."

"But I trusted Percy. I told him things I've never told another soul—not even George. I don't understand how he could betray me like this."

Reaching over, Happy gently patted Lula Mae's hand. "Because he's a pig-headed old goat," she said.

My appetite faltered at the sight of Lula Mae's sagging shoulders and puffy, red eyes. "How about a game of dominoes?" I suggested, hoping to cheer her up.

Both Happy and Lula Mae turned to stare at me as if I'd just gotten out of the nut house.

"It was only a suggestion," I said weakly, and got up to clear the table.

They were still sitting at the table discussing all the ways they planned to make Percy's life miserable when I finished with the dishes. I could think of better ways to spend my time. I grabbed one of the mysteries I'd picked up at the library and headed upstairs to match wits with the sleuth.

It was a little after eight when Happy tapped on my door and informed me that Lula Mae was ready to go home. Being the dutiful daughter that I am, and not wanting to be responsible for unleashing the two of them on the streets at night, I tugged on my sneakers and offered to drive her home.

As I was going out the door, Happy shoved a list of items we needed from the grocery store into my hands. "And don't even think about coming back here with any of that imitation cheese stuff you bought last time. Nobody can make decent macaroni and cheese with that stuff."

"How about I just buy some of that macaroni and cheese that comes in those little, cardboard boxes?"

She shot me a withering look before slamming the door in my face.

On the trip across town, Lula Mae huddled on her side of the truck, absolutely silent. All my attempts to lighten her spirits failed. It wasn't until we pulled into her driveway that she finally spoke, "Who told you about Percy and Camilla?"

I hemmed and hawed a few minutes, then broke down and gave her an abbreviated version of last night's events.

"I see." Unshed tears glistened in her eyes. Squaring her shoulders, she crawled out of the truck. My offer to walk her to the door was turned down. "Don't worry about me. I'll be just fine. You just run along home now. Happy will be expecting you."

I hated seeing her so dispirited. "Well, call us if you need anything."

The nearest grocery store was only a few blocks away. The problem was: the sight of all that food awakened my appetite. After stowing the groceries safely away in the bed of my truck, I made a beeline for Bob's, where they make the best milkshakes in town. Thick and creamy, just the way I like them.

Too bad I didn't have the foresight to stay there all night.

As I pulled into the driveway with my load of groceries, Happy was climbing into her beat-up, old LTD, which I'd nicknamed the Blue Bomber when she'd refused to trade it in on a newer model. She had on a pair of purple sweats, and her hair stuck up in tufts about her head as if she hadn't taken time to comb it.

Alarmed by her appearance, I quickly killed the engine and scrambled out of the truck. "Where do you think you're going at this time of the night?" I asked, knowing she was practically blind at night.

"Thank goodness you're back." Not bothering to answer my question, she scooted across the smooth, vinyl seat to the passenger's side of the car. "Don't just stand there with your mouth hanging open," she said, "get in. Lula Mae needs us."

That got my attention. I hurried inside and stashed the groceries in the kitchen, then ran back to the car. As I crawled inside, I forgot the seat was pulled up to accommodate her short stature and smashed my knees against the steering column. "Ouch," I cried out, then readjusted the seat to handle my five foot, eight inch frame.

As soon as we were on the road, I demanded an explanation. "What's wrong with Lula Mae? Is she sick? Does she need us to drive her to the hospital?"

"No, it's nothing like that." She seemed flustered. "It's

Camilla Davenport. She's been—"

"What!" I hit the brake, slowed down to the posted speed, then proceeded to yell, "You mean you scared me half out of my wits, let me drive like a lunatic and endanger our lives, as well as the lives of everyone on the road, all because Lula Mae's still upset over this Camilla Davenport nonsense?"

"If you'd shut your mouth and let me finish," she said, in that tone that says you'd better do as I say, or else.

I managed to curb the inclination to tell her . . . well, never mind what I wanted to tell her.

"That's more like it." She nodded in satisfaction. There was a long pause, then the words spewed out of her like a round of buckshot, "Camilla Davenport's dead."

The blood seemed to drain from my head in a whoosh. I steered toward the curb, turned off the engine, then rested my forehead against the cold, hard steering wheel. "What do you mean—dead?"

"What do you think I mean? Dead. Gone. Kaput." She paused long enough for her words to sink in, then went on to add, "Sue Ann called me. She said Mary Beth heard from her younger sister that the housekeeper found Camilla when she got home from the movies. Looks like someone bashed her head in with a fireplace poker."

My eyes shot open. "But that sounds like murder."

"You bet it does." Happy mouth was set in a grim line.

This couldn't be happening. Someone I knew—murdered.

As I pulled back onto the road, silence settled over us. Though neither of us seemed ready to acknowledge the fact, we both knew Camilla hadn't been dining alone.

It was a relief to finally reach Lula Mae's house. Before the car came to a complete stop, Happy flung open the door and began to scoot out. I reached over and grabbed her arm. "Did Sue Ann go into any more details about what happened?"

Her eyebrows shot up. "Like, was anyone found with her? And do the police have a motive or a suspect in custody?"

"Something like that, yeah."

"Nope. But then, that's why we're here." She jerked her arm free. "To break the news to Lula Mae, then get our butts over there and find out what in the dickens is going on." She hopped out of the car and took off for the house.

"Oh, no." I flung open my own door and went after her. "We are not going over there. The police will be there collecting evidence. You can just get on the phone and call up one of your friends. I'm sure she'll be able to fill you in on all the juicy details."

She tossed me a knowing smile, then shuffled up the steps and banged on Lula Mae's door. "It's me, Lula Mae, open up."

While Happy filled Lula Mae in on what was happening, I paced around the living room, still unable to believe that someone I knew—had talked to that very day—had actually been murdered. I kept waiting for someone to say, "Hey, it was just a bad joke. Nobody's been murdered. What kind of town do you think we live in?"

"What about Percy?" Lula Mae wanted to know. "Is he dead too?" She slapped a hand to her throat and moaned. "It's all my fault. I should never have said all that stuff about wishing he was dead."

"Get hold of yourself, Lula Mae," Happy said. "No one said anything about Percy being dead."

She slumped down in a chair. "Then he's not dead?"

"Sue Ann didn't say anything about another body, so I assume he's fine."

"But you don't know for sure?"

"He's fine, Lula Mae," Happy said in a firm voice. "Now get in there and change out of those pajamas so we can get over to Camilla's."

"We are not going over there," I said.

Ignoring me, Lula Mae leaped up and plowed toward her bedroom faster than the speed of light. She was back a few minutes later with her hair combed, wearing a blue cotton dress. She grabbed her purse off the table. "I'm ready," she said.

Like a broken record, I repeated, "We are not going over there."

The two of them stood there like lions, claws in the ready position, waiting for me to give in peacefully. "Look, Lula Mae," I said, trying another tactic, "the man was two-timing you with the deceased. Do you really think we should go over there?"

For a second, Lula Mae's resolve seem to falter. Then, it bounced back. "It's our Christian duty to help if we can."

"Well, I'm not driving you." I plopped down on the couch and folded my arms. "I'm not doing it," I repeated. "So just forget it."

"She's driving you all right," Happy declared. "Or she's not going to be eating any more of my home cooked meals. Ever."

After a few minutes of stony silence, I gave in and drove them to Camilla's.

CHAPTER SEVEN

The sidewalk in front of Camilla's house was jammed with people. Two police cars and a coroner's van blocked the drive. We found a parking spot a few houses down, then hurried back to join the throng gathered on the sidewalk.

Mary Beth, a tall, thin woman in a tacky yellow robe, broke loose from the group and rushed over to greet us, no doubt seeking a fresh audience. "I just can't believe it," she said. "Something this horrible happening right here in our own neighborhood. Why, none of us will be safe until this monster is caught and put behind bars where he belongs."

I glanced toward the sprawling house, now ablaze with lights. Though it was one of the older homes in the area, it was well maintained. Double entrance doors, floor-length windows, and a center gable with a fanlight window contributed to its classic charm.

Tom Jenkins, packed into a pair of white, cotton shorts and a bright orange T-shirt, spotted us and nudged his way over. "No doubt the killer must've been after money." He swiped a hand over his balding head. "Camilla had a habit of keeping lots of cash lying around. Her 'getting away' money, she called it. Not to mention all that jewelry she insisted on keeping at home. I must have told her a million times. 'Come down to the bank and rent yourself a safety deposit box.' "

"Do the police have any idea who killed her?" I asked.

He shrugged. "Not as far as I know. But Mary Beth said she

saw a brown Chevy parked in the driveway earlier. Maybe it belonged to the killer."

I swiveled around, hoping Lula Mae hadn't heard this last remark. But from the look on her face, chances were good she had. "I'm sure there must be lots of brown Chevies around town." She folded her arms across her chest and glared at us. "Just because Percy happens to own one, doesn't mean he killed anybody."

Tom had the good sense to back away.

Suddenly, the crowd quieted. All eyes riveted on Camilla's front porch as a tall, well-built man with a clump of short, brown hair emerged. My stomach began to churn. I should've realized that Steven—make that Lieutenant Griggs—would be handling this case. Clamping my eyes shut, I willed him to go away.

Beside me I heard Happy yell, "Yoo-hoo." Then, yielding to her tendency to act before thinking, she went galloping off across the lawn.

The young officer who'd been leaning against his squad car, darted out to intercept her. But she was ready for him. Flinging up her purse, she rapped the startled young man over the head with it. Temporarily stunned, he staggered backward.

I decided to hightail it over there before she got herself into even more trouble. By the time I pushed through the crowd, the over-excited cop already had his handcuffs out. When Steven realized what was happening, he yelled for the young officer to let Happy through.

With obvious reluctance, the officer put away his cuffs.

Happy wagged her tongue at him. Before she could get too cocky, I snagged her arm and dragged her back toward the sidewalk. She immediately began to bellow, "Let go of me," and tried to jerk free.

I hung on tighter. "Are you nuts?"

"I'll show you who's nuts." She flung up her purse as she had done with the young cop, ready to use it on me.

"You two stop fighting and get over here," Steven ordered from the porch, putting an end to our tug of war.

As soon as I released her arm, Happy tossed me a smug grin, then sashayed over to join Steven on the porch. Against my better judgment, I followed her.

The instant my feet hit the steps, Steven's serious gray eyes settled on me. "You do realize this is a crime scene? And that neither one of you has any business being here."

"We are well aware of the situation, young man," Happy said, gripping her purse tightly. "Why else do you think we're here?"

His attention shifted in her direction. "To be honest, Mrs. Spencer, I have no idea why you're here." He rested his muscular frame against the side of the house. "Care to enlighten me?"

"Don't go getting uppity with me, young man," Happy said. "I remember when you were nothing more than—"

"What my mother is so graciously trying to say is," I said, taking charge of the conversation, "we'd be happy to cooperate with your investigation in any way we can."

The offer seemed to take him by surprise. "And what makes you think I need your help?"

Happy rolled her eyes upward. "Because, Steven J. Griggs, you happen to be investigating the death of Camilla Davenport."

For a fleeting moment, I got the distinct impression she intended to rap a little sense into his head with that weapon she calls a purse. But for once, good judgment seemed to prevail. "It just so happens that Camilla Davenport was at our garden center this morning and—"

"I hardly see where that is—" he began.

"As I was saying." Happy's voice rose by several decibels, drowning out his words. "My daughter overheard Camilla mention that she was expecting a dinner guest this evening. Now, I'm sure that if you just let us inside, we can get to the bottom of this unfortunate situation in no time."

"I'm afraid, Mrs. Spencer, that's just not possible."

"Sure it is," she replied, then slipped right past him into the house.

He hurried after her. So naturally, I followed. By the time we caught up with her, Happy's sassy demeanor was gone. One glance in the direction of the living room told me why. Camilla Davenport's body lay face down next to the piano. Her silver hair was matted, and now an ugly shade of rust. On the oak floor beside her lay the fireplace poker that, according to Mary Beth, was the murder weapon.

Ignoring our presence, a slightly pudgy, middle-aged man shuffled about the room snapping pictures of the body, while another dusted for prints.

Never having actually been that close to a dead body before—outside the funeral home, of course—my knees began to feel a little wobbly. Happy didn't seem to be faring much better. Steven seemed to realize our predicament and hustled us outside, guiding us toward a set of wrought iron chairs at the end of the porch. Grateful for the support, we slumped down. Steven stood nearby, waiting patiently, giving us time to recover.

Happy managed to rally first. "I didn't see Percy inside." She cast an accusing look at Steven. "What have you done with him"

"The dinner guest, I presume."

"Who else would I be talking about, young man?" She sounded cranky.

A speculative look crossed his face.

"I know what you're thinking," I said, "but you're wrong."

"How can you be so sure?"

"Because . . . because I know my aunt's fiancé would never

kill anybody."

"Fiancé." He looked startled. "Didn't her husband pass away not too long ago?"

The fire was back in Happy's eyes. "What's that got to do with anything?"

"Nothing. Nothing at all." He pulled a battered notebook from his pocket. "What can you tell me about this Mr.—" He waited for one of us to supply a name.

"Moss," I reluctantly said.

Happy scrambled to her feet. "We need to get home. I have a roast that needs to go into the oven."

"At this time of night?" He reached over and gently restrained her. "What can you tell me about this Moss fellow?"

Resigned, Happy plopped back down. "Not much, I'm afraid. The man seems to have popped up out of nowhere. I must've told Lula Mae at least a hundred times, 'You don't really know anything about this guy. He could be an ax murderer, for all we know. Or, some lunatic who slices up women.' "

Steven took a deep breath, then said, "Why don't we start with a description."

I fielded that question. "He's about five-six, around one hundred ninety pounds, has dingy white hair and blue eyes."

He flipped to a page in his notebook and stopped to read an entry. "Your description matches one we have of a suspect who was seen fleeing the premises earlier tonight." He uncapped a pen. "Do either one of you ladies have an address for Mr. Moss?"

Happy's earlier cockiness seemed to evaporate. "He's renting the old Carmichael place out on River Road," she said quietly.

Summoning one of his men, Steven handed him the address and told him to take a couple of guys and check it out.

"Just because Percy was having dinner with Camilla," I pointed out, "doesn't mean he killed her." I nearly fell over with surprise. Had those words really come out of my mouth?

"She's right." Happy jumped on the bandwagon. "I'm sure there are lots of people who didn't get along with Camilla. One of them probably did her in."

He frowned. "As I recall, you don't get along all that well with Camilla Davenport."

Her eyes narrowed. "It's best not to rile me, young man."

Pulling one of those cop techniques out of the bag, he waited patiently, letting the silence stretch between them. Finally, she caved. "So Camilla Davenport wasn't one of my favorite people. Chances are—she wasn't one of yours either."

He winced. "You're right about that."

Rumor had it that Camilla had once rammed his car for taking what she considered, "her parking space." Of course, that was long before he became a cop; otherwise, he might've thrown her in jail and tossed away the key.

Before he could get around to dismissing us, I thought I'd get in a few questions of my own. "Mr. Jenkins told us the killer was probably after Camilla's jewelry and all that cash she had stashed around the place."

Horizontal creases marred his forehead. "We haven't determined if anything is missing yet." For a brief instant our gazes locked. A faint spark of some long-forgotten heat began to stir between us.

Suddenly, Happy grabbed my arm and pulled me to my feet. "Well, if you're done with your questions, young man, we'll be on our way."

Before he could offer an objection, she hauled me down the steps. After retrieving Lula Mae from the clutches of Betsy Seymour, she herded us both toward the car.

As we pulled away from the curb, Lula Mae leaned forward, resting her arms on the back of the seat. "Well, what did you find out? Did someone really bash in Camilla's skull? Where's

Percy? Is he under arrest?"

Happy shifted around to face her. "The police weren't being very helpful. Someone bashed in Camilla's skull all right. That much we saw for ourselves. And it appears a wad of money and some of Camilla's jewelry is missing. So maybe—"

"May be missing," I corrected her.

She ignored me. "Robbery might be a motive. And Percy's not under arrest, he's—gone."

Lula Mae looked confused. "Gone where?"

I glanced at her in the rear view mirror. "Run off with Camilla's money, most likely," I told her.

Lula Mae straightened her spine. "Percy may be a two-timing lout, but I can't believe he'd kill anyone."

I opened my mouth to set her straight, but Happy shot me a look that made me change my mind.

"Don't worry," Happy said. "I'm sure once the police locate Percy and hear his side of the story, they'll realize he had nothing to do with her death."

"Oh, dear." Lula Mae pressed a hand to the base of her throat. "You don't think the killer might have . . ."

"I'm sure Percy's fine. The coward—" Happy cleared her throat. "I mean—the poor man probably got scared and decided to hide out until the police make an arrest. What we need to do is find him, convince him to talk to the police. He may be the only one who can identify the killer."

"Wake up call," I said. "Dead woman. Killer on the loose. Anyone see a problem here?"

They both ignored me. "Think about it, Lula Mae," Happy urged. "Where would Percy hide out? Where would he feel safe?"

"Hold on a minute," I said. "We're not chasing after Percy. That's a job for the police. They have the resources to—"

Happy crossed her arms and glared at me. "The police don't know the first thing about Percy. Lula Mae knows his habits.

How he thinks. If anyone can find him, she can."

My blood pressure shot up ten notches. I jerked the car to the side of the road, switched off the engine, then twisted sideways to face them. "There's a killer on the loose. We can't go running around, sticking our noses into police business. It's not safe."

Happy snatched the keys out of the ignition, hopped out, and popped open the trunk. She returned with a baseball bat. "Does this make you feel any safer?"

"Put that back in the trunk," I commanded. "We are not a bunch of two bit thugs out to break some sap's legs."

Happy shrugged. "I was just trying to make you feel better," she grumbled, returning the bat to the trunk.

Silence hung in the air as she slid into the car. Finally, I said, "Why do I get the feeling you two know something you're not telling me?"

Happy pursed her lips and stared out the front windshield. In the back seat, Lula Mae fiddled with the contents of her purse.

"Out with it," I demanded.

"Okay." Happy swiveled around to face me. "Percy might've . . . borrowed . . . a few of your uncle's things."

A feeling of dread spread through me. "What things?"

Tears began to trickle down Lula Mae's face. When she spoke, her voice was barely a whisper. "His grandfather's watch. His good cuff links. Maybe a few gold and silver coins he had in the lock box."

"So, it's entirely possible Camilla caught him pocketing her jewelry and threatened to call the police. Only he killed her before she could make the call."

Lula Mae leaned back in her seat, putting as much distance between us as possible. "Percy may be a thief, but I don't think he's capable of violence."

I rolled my eyes heavenward, amazed by her naiveté. "I don't suppose you reported any of this to the police."

She shook her head. "I wanted to give him a chance to return your uncle's things."

She looked so miserable, I didn't have the heart to scold her. I just cranked up the engine and chauffeured them around town. But no matter how much the two of them protested, I had no intention of confronting Percy if we found him. I'd simply head for the nearest phone, call the police, and let them take it from there.

In the end, none of Lula Mae's ideas about Percy's whereabouts panned out, so we called it a night and headed home. As soon as we crossed the threshold, the two of them trotted upstairs. That suited me fine. Grabbing a can of soda from the kitchen, I drifted out to the front porch and plopped down in the swing.

The night was a little too warm for comfort, the air dripping with moisture. In the distance, I heard the howl of a dog and the whistle of a train. Percy was out there somewhere. Alone. Afraid of being discovered. Because he murdered Camilla? Or because he knew who had?

I had to admit, the robbery part sounded entirely plausible; the murder part—well, like Lula Mae, I was having a hard time wrapping my mind around the idea.

My musings were cut short when a police cruiser pulled into the drive. Though no lights were flashing to attract neighbors, the sight sent a chill racing up my spine.

CHAPTER EIGHT

The car door opened and Lieutenant Griggs climbed out. "Mind some company?" he asked. Not waiting for an answer, he mounted the steps and plopped down in one of the wicker chairs, which abutted the wall.

"How about a soda?" I offered.

He nodded. "Sounds good."

When I returned with his drink, he was leaning back in the chair with his eyes closed. For a moment, I thought he might have fallen asleep. Then, as if he sensed he was being watched, his eyes popped open. "Sorry. It's been a long night."

I handed him his soda and returned to the swing. "Have any luck finding Percy?"

"Afraid not." He snapped open the can and took a sip. "You have any idea where he might be hiding out?"

"Your guess is as good as mine."

He sighed. "I was afraid you'd say that. I'll check with Lula Mae in the morning, see if she has any suggestions."

Far be it from me to disillusion him. "That's probably a good idea."

"How's she holding up?"

Falling apart, I wanted to say. I settled for, "About as well as can be expected."

We sat there awhile, sipping our drinks, listening to the squeak of the swing. "It's getting pretty late," I finally said. "Won't your fiancée be getting worried?"

"Sissy." He supplied the name.

I arched my brows. "Is that her name?"

"You know perfectly well—"

"What kind of name is that?" I interrupted. "Sounds like something you'd call a skinny little wimp."

A small grin tugged at the corners of his mouth. "Not a very accurate description of Sissy Holmes."

I couldn't hold back a grin. Sissy Holmes was a petite blonde who went after what she wanted with a passion. And if anyone didn't willingly bend to her wishes, they could usually be persuaded to see things her way once she flashed around some of her daddy's money.

"The fact is," he said, "we've decided to call off the engagement."

"Your idea or hers?"

He gave a mirthless chuckle. "Does it matter?"

"I guess not. It's just that . . . I hadn't heard about—"

"Now there's a first."

My hackles started to rise. "What's that supposed to mean?"

"Come on. We both know your mother."

"Are you implying my mother is one of those women who sticks her nose into everybody's business?"

He threw up a hand to halt my words. "I'm not implying anything. It's just"—he treaded carefully—"we both know your mother happens to have lots of friends in this town. Friends who make a habit of sharing information with her about mutual acquaintances."

He had a point. Happy's friends probably had supplied her with all the sordid details. Only, Steven J. Griggs is kind of a sore subject between us. Has been ever since my senior year of high school when Steven and I had fallen madly in love and made plans to marry. Only the closer our wedding day got, the colder my feet seemed to get. Two days before the wedding, they galloped right off to Atlanta.

And stayed there for almost six months.

By the time I came to my senses and forced them to march back home, Steven's feet had taken him off to college to study criminal law.

Forcing my thoughts to return to the here and now, I jumped up and went to lean against the porch railing. Across the street, the kitchen light winked on. Old man McCarthy must be raiding the refrigerator again. Finally, I turned around to face Steven. "So what happened?" I asked, trying to keep my voice steady. "I thought you two were made for each other."

"It seems she wasn't interested in being married to a cop."

"Let me guess," I said. "She wanted you to go to work for her daddy."

"Bingo."

"Not a bad idea. A few years in the trenches and you could wind up a rich man."

"As long as I danced to her daddy's tune," he said. "But you know me. All I ever wanted to be was a cop. My dad was a cop. His dad was a cop. You could say: it runs in our blood."

"There's still time. Sissy could come to her senses and realize what a great guy she's giving up." Realizing my choice of words might give him the wrong impression, I quickly backpedaled, "I mean—"

"I know what you mean." He stood up. "The problem is, I'm not sure I want her to come to her senses anymore."

What happened next is kind of hard to explain. It seemed as if some invisible wave of energy rolled out of his body and collided with mine. An intense heat swept through every inch of my body. It felt so wonderful; I never wanted it to end.

A strange look passed over his face. "Goodnight, Katie," he said softly, then plodded down the steps to his car.

CHAPTER NINE

Splatters of warm sunlight filled the kitchen. The aroma of cinnamon oozed through the air. I traced the smell to a platter of cinnamon buns on the counter. Judging from the numerous circles of white frosting left behind, I'd say Happy and Lula Mae had already eaten their share and had gone off to take care of errands of their own.

That suited me fine because I had this overwhelming urge to do a little snooping and wasn't too keen on the idea of them tagging along.

After gulping down a cup of coffee and a couple of rolls, I put in a call to Jolene, our part-time worker at the garden center, and asked her to open up. Always eager for the extra hours, she quickly agreed to work as long as we needed her. After hanging up the phone, I snatched my purse off the counter and set off for the old Carmichael place, looking for Percy.

Since his car wasn't under the carport when I drove past, I had to assume he was still in hiding. Under normal circumstances, I would've simply marched up the walkway and knocked on the front door or peeked through a few windows, but with a police car parked down the street, I moved on to Plan B. Taking the next right, I drove around the block and parked next to an undeveloped lot behind his house. Then I got out and trudged through waist high weeds until I reached the back of his property.

Unfortunately, the six foot hedge of holly that rimmed his

backyard proved almost impossible to penetrate. Not wanting to give up, I plodded along until I found a gap in the shrubbery, which looked promising. Turning sideways, I managed to squeeze through the narrow opening and popped out on the other side with only a few minor scratches.

A thick carpet of St. Augustine grass muted my approach and gave me time to study the house, one of those sprawling, ranch style places with a wooden deck tacked onto the back. Always a good sign—there were no barking dogs to announce my presence, and no curious faces appeared at any of the windows.

I clambered up the cypress steps and tried the rear door. No surprise. It was locked. I moved over to check out the windows that ran along the back. At the third one, I lucked out. There was almost an inch gap along the bottom. Since the window was too high to climb through without a boost, I dragged over one of the heavy redwood chairs scattered across the deck. In no time at all, I had the screen off and the window fully open.

Before I could lose my nerve, I wiggled through the narrow opening and landed in a sparkling white bathtub, which was surrounded by the most disgusting pink tiles I'd ever seen. After giving myself a pat on the back for still being able to perform such an athletic feat, I shoved open the glass paneled shower door and found myself staring down the barrel of a gun.

Believe me, I'm no fool. I froze in place like one of those concrete statues we sell down at the Flower Patch. "In here," the fresh-faced officer from last night's fiasco called.

Footsteps pounded down the hall. A second later, Steven shot through the doorway. Taking one look at my bloodless face, he ordered the rookie to holster his weapon. "It's okay, Joe. I'll take over here. You go help Fred."

Noting how badly Joe's hand shook as he put away the weapon, I felt a little woozy. His face turned crimson as he sputtered out an apology. Duty done, he made a quick escape, leaving me alone with his angry boss.

"I wondered when you'd show up." Horizontal creases marred his forehead. "This is the second call we've had this morning about a possible break-in."

"Mrs. Peterson," I guessed.

"The one and only."

Mrs. Peterson was our local birdwatcher, snoop, and general pest of the police department. Last year, she was convinced aliens had landed on the beach and were secretly planning to take over the town.

"I'm surprised you even bothered to check out her story."

"We always respond to calls from our citizens," he said, "no matter how farfetched they sound."

"I'll remember that next time an alien lands on my doorstep."

He ignored my attempt at humor. "Mrs. Peterson told us she saw Percy carrying a couple of suitcases out to his car last night." His eyes narrowed. "And she did steer us right about Lula Mae and Happy."

Goosebumps popped out on my arms. "What about them?"

"Joe caught them snooping around the place this morning." He reached into his pocket and pulled out a key. "He took this off them. Though they claim they didn't need it, because the front door was open."

"Why those two old—"

"What I should do is haul the three of you down to the station and hold you there until this investigation is over. All I need is a bunch of amateur sleuths running around town interfering in my investigation."

"You wouldn't do that," I said, accepting the hand he held out and stepping out of the tub with as much dignity as I could muster.

"Don't tempt me." He rested his back against the sink. "Want

59

to tell me why you're trespassing on Mr. Moss's property?"

Was it my imagination, or did the room suddenly shrink? The woodsy scent of his cologne teased my senses, making it impossible to concentrate. "I thought I might find . . ." I shook my head, trying to clear it. "I wanted to figure out . . ." Anger surged through my veins. "If you knew what he did to Lula Mae, you wouldn't be harassing me like this."

He threw up a hand. "Spare me the Percy-done-me-wrong speech. I've already heard it." His tone hardened. "And, no, you cannot look around for any of your uncle's stuff."

I shrugged, decided to come at it from a different angle. "You know, Percy was having dinner with Camilla last night. Maybe he knows who killed her, and he's gone into hiding because he's afraid the killer might come after him next."

"What makes you so sure he didn't kill her?"

How could I explain it to him? "It just doesn't feel right."

He rolled his eyes. "It doesn't feel right, huh?" He nodded toward the door. "Go on, get out of here before I change my mind and haul you down to the station."

My mama didn't raise no dummy. I squeezed past the man and double-timed it down the hallway. Since I couldn't very well return the way I'd come—not with the shaky-handed rookie watching my every move—I was forced to plod around the block. As soon as I reached my truck, I climbed in and set off for the garden center to have a heart-to-heart with my dear old mother and aunt.

Apparently, they must have sensed me coming, because Jolene told me they'd left not more than five minutes ago. I hurried back to my truck, then cruised the area, hoping to catch a glimpse of Happy's car. I was on the verge of giving up when I spotted it outside Bessie's Kitchen, a moderately priced diner that serves the best barbecue in town.

Much to the delight of the driver glued to my bumper, I

slammed on the brakes and veered right, sliding into the empty space beside the Blue Bomber. I cut the engine and headed inside.

With the breakfast rush over, I had no trouble locating the guilty pair. They were packed into a booth near the kitchen with Bessie, the owner of this fine establishment. I plowed through the empty tables to where they were sitting. "I want to have a word with you two."

Happy looked up, her face a mask of child-like innocence. "What about, dear?"

"About how you two got thrown out of Percy's this morning, for starters." I loomed at the edge of the booth, towering over them.

"Where on earth did you get such a ridiculous idea?" Lula Mae said, her expression an identical copy of Happy's.

I suddenly wondered why the two of them had never taken up acting—they definitely had the talent for it.

"Hmm." Happy pursed her lips together and stared at me. "Yes, dear, that is an interesting question. Why would you think we were there? Unless . . ." She waited for me to hang myself.

Searing heat toasted my face as my gaze flicked back and forth between the two. "Uh, well, it's like this—"

"You know because you got caught snooping yourself." Happy let out a crow of delight.

"So I was there. That's doesn't explain what you two were doing there."

"We only went over there," Lula Mae said, "because we wanted to get your Uncle George's stuff back." The false eyelashes she'd taken to wearing since she'd met Percy fluttered in my direction. "Surely you can understand that."

Bessie had listened to the exchange with obvious amusement. Realizing I wasn't going to be leaving anytime soon, she cheerfully slid her ample girth over to make room for me on the smooth, vinyl bench. "Sid," she called to the skinny black guy behind the counter, "how about bringing over another cup of coffee."

As soon as my coffee arrived, I took a sip, then got down to business. "So, did the two of you manage to come up with anything useful?"

"You bet your booties we did." Happy slapped her purse on the table and proceeded to extract several envelopes.

"Percy's mail." I couldn't believe it. "You stole Percy's mail?"

"Not stole, dear. Borrowed," Happy said. "There is a difference."

Right. The same way Percy *borrowed* Uncle George's stuff. "You do realize that taking someone's mail is a federal offense," I said. "And Steven is going to have your hide for interfering in his investigation."

Happy snorted. "Him. He's just a kid. What does he know?"

"He may seem like a kid to you." I was forced to assume the adult role. "But he happens to be in charge of this investigation and I don't think he's going to be too happy when he finds out you stole Percy's mail."

"Enough." Lula Mae rapped a teaspoon against her cup. "You," she said, glaring at me, "be quiet and let your mother speak."

I didn't like it, but I did as I was told and shut up.

Eyes glowing with excitement, Happy opened the first envelope and shoved its contents toward me. "You'll notice that Percy's made quite a few calls to this here number in Mobile." She jabbed a finger at the number listed. "We haven't had time to check it out yet, but we'll get around to it soon."

"I don't see how that—" I began, before Happy's stony expression short-circuited my mouth.

"Now, the reason we happen to be at Bessie's is because of this." She handed me the contents of the second envelope, a credit card statement. "Notice all those charges made right here at Bessie's."

"I was just telling your mama," Bessie said, "that Percy comes in here all the time. Sometimes alone. But mostly he has some woman hanging on his arm. Of course," she frowned, "I had no idea he was sweet on Lula Mae 'cause he ain't never brung her in here that I can recall."

Tears started to trickle down Lula Mae's face. Avoiding her eyes, I grabbed my coffee cup and took a few gulps. Searing heat scorched the roof of my mouth, but I ignored the pain and pretended everything was fine.

Seeing the misery on Lula Mae's face caused Happy to lose some of her spunk. "Don't fret, Lula Mae. I'm sure Percy has a logical explanation for his absence. When we find him—"

"What?" Lula Mae sat up straighter. "He'll give me back George's stuff and we'll go on with the wedding as if nothing has happened? Surely you don't believe that I'd marry that lout now."

My heart ached for Lula Mae. She'd always been too trusting, so ready to see the best in others. I suppose that's why Uncle George had always been so protective of her. Then to have a creep like Percy take advantage of her—to destroy that child-like innocence. The man deserved to be locked up.

"When we find Percy," Lula Mae went on, clutching her pocketbook to her chest, "I intend to give him a piece of my mind for humiliating me in front of the whole town. He'd better pray the police get to him first."

I don't think I'd ever seen Lula Mae so mad.

"Hon, you've got to calm down." Bessie leaned forward and patted Lula Mae's hand. "No man's worth all that trouble."

"She's right, Lula Mae," Happy said. "There's no sense getting yourself all worked up. When we find Percy, we'll just sit him down and ask him, nice and calmly—what in the dickens he thought he was doing prancing around town like some California playboy."

"But first, we'll ask him if he knows who killed Camilla," I said.

Happy gave me "the look," and I shut up.

While Lula Mae made an effort to calm down, a young couple finished their meal and headed for the register. Making her apologies, Bessie trotted off to take their money.

"Was this all you found?" I asked, indicating the papers on the table.

Happy nodded. "We were hoping to find the stuff Percy took from Lula Mae, but that kid from last night ran us out of there before we had a chance to search the place."

"I don't know what that boy thought he was doing," Lula Mae said huffily. "It's not like we were robbing the place. We had a key."

Thankfully, Happy had already scribbled down the names of Percy's dinner companions before Bessie had to return to work. "I suppose our next move is to check out the women on your list." I nodded toward the rumpled paper next to Happy's cup. "Maybe one of them has some idea where Percy is hiding out."

"*Our* next move," they replied in unison.

"Of course." I stood up. "You don't think I'm letting you two run around town on your own, do you?"

CHAPTER TEN

The first name on Happy's list was Lucille Crandell. She was a big-boned woman with coal black hair and clear, cream-colored skin, who lived in a rambling Victorian near the end of Main. She seemed surprised to see us, but recovered quickly enough, ushering us into a room stuffed with antiques. We politely accepted her offer of iced tea and oatmeal cookies "fresh from the oven."

After we suffered through countless minutes of boring chatter, the conversation finally turned in the direction we wanted. At the mention of Percy's name, Lucille's face began to flame. She lowered her head and began to brush imaginary crumbs from her lap. "I don't believe I know the gentleman."

"That's funny," Happy said, scooting to the edge of her chair, "because Bessie was just telling us that she's seen you come into her place with him at least a half a dozen times."

Lucille grabbed the pitcher of tea from the coffee table and began to refill her glass. "Evidently, she must have me confused with someone else."

"I don't think so." Lula Mae sat up straighter. "What I'd like to know is, how long have you being running around town with my fiancé?"

Tea sloshed over the rim of Lucille's glass, spilling onto the coffee table. Snatching up a napkin, she began to dab at the spreading liquid. "Oh, Lula Mae, I'm so sorry. I had no idea things had gone that far." Her eyes seemed to beg for understanding. "I came by the garden center a few days ago to warn you about Percy, but when I saw all those people . . . I just lost my nerve. Will you ever be able to forgive me?"

The torrent of words pouring out of Lucille's mouth seemed to confuse Lula Mae.

"What exactly did you want to warn her about?" I asked.

She gave me a brief glance, then turned her attention back to Lula Mae. "It's just that, when I first met Percy he seemed so nice. So wonderful. Almost like an answer to my prayers." Her cornflower blue eyes clouded. "But when he found out that Tom didn't leave me with anything except this house and a couple of beat up old cars—"

"He dumped you," Happy guessed.

Lucille glanced around the room taking in the collection of fine furnishings she'd gathered over the years. "First he tried to convince me to unload all this 'junk,' as he put it, and use the money to finance some business venture he just knew would make us a fortune."

"But when he found out you had no intention of parting with a single piece," Happy tried again.

"He dumped me," Lucille confirmed.

Tension radiated from Lula Mae, who sat beside me on the couch, clutching her purse tightly against her abdomen. "I can't believe Percy thought he could get away with two-timing me. Not in this town."

"Three-timing you," I corrected. "If you count Camilla."

Lula Mae turned to glare at me, before continuing, "Percy seemed like such a kind, generous man. I thought he really cared about me. I had no idea he had such . . . loose morals."

"Lula Mae, I've known you since we were girls playing hopscotch on the school grounds," Lucille said. "You can't let loneliness blind you to the truth. Percy Moss is not an honorable man. He only wanted to get hold of your money."

Lula Mae stood up, her chin lifted proudly in the air. " 'Judge not, that ye be not judged.' That's what the good book says. That's what I'm trying my best to do. Only it's a lot harder to do than I thought." On that note, she marched out of the room.

Happy started to follow Lula Mae, but I motioned her to stay put. "What can you tell us about Percy's connection to Camilla?"

Lucille gave me a blank look. "I didn't know there was a connection until you just mentioned it."

"Come on now," Happy said, getting into the swing of things. "Everyone in town knows Percy was hitting her up for money to open some business. Same as he did with you."

Lucille's eyes narrowed. "I hope you're not implying that Percy had anything to do with Camilla's murder. Sure, he was probably after her money. Everybody in town knew she was loaded. But just because the man's a thief and a louse, it doesn't mean he's a killer."

Where had I heard those words? "No one's accusing Percy of—" I began.

"Look." Lucille got to her feet. "I've enjoyed the visit, but I have some business I need to take care of in town."

Happy scrambled to her feet. "Is it okay if I use your bathroom before we go? My bladder ain't what it used to be."

While Happy took care of business, I sat back down. "You would've saved us all a lot of trouble if you would've come clean about Percy before he had a chance to break Lula Mae's heart."

Lucille clamped her lips together and stared at something across the room.

"This disappearing act of Percy's makes him look guilty of a whole lot more than being a con artist. I don't want Lula Mae's good name dragged through the mud just because she . . . ." I couldn't bring myself to use the word loved. ". . . cared about the man."

Lucille's gaze riveted in on me. "I don't want Lula Mae's reputation ruined any more than you do. That's why I came to the garden center that day to warn her."

"But you didn't have the courage to come inside and tell her what you knew."

She lifted her chin. "She wouldn't have listened. The man already had her bamboozled."

Before I could think of a snappy comeback, Happy waltzed back into the room, looking entirely too satisfied with herself. Lucille hopped to her feet and hustled us toward the door. We nearly had a three-way pile up by the front door when Happy came to an abrupt stop, spun around, and said, "By the way, Lucille, the police are looking for Percy. You wouldn't happen to know where he's hiding out, would you?"

All color drained from Lucille's face. She shrugged. "How should I know? I'm not the man's keeper."

Happy regarded her thoughtfully. "Well, give us a call if you hear from him. If he didn't bash Camilla's head in, maybe he saw who did."

"Sure thing." She practically shoved us out the door, then slammed it shut behind us.

"What was that all about?" I asked when we reached the car.

"Nothing," Happy said as she climbed into the front seat. "I just wanted to see if she was being honest with us."

"And?" I prompted, hanging on to the door so she couldn't close it.

"And now I know she's not."

I could feel my blood pressure shoot up. "And you know this because . . ."

"Nothing I can put my finger on, but I'm sure she's lying."

"Of course she's lying," Lula Mae piped up from the back

seat. "Percy wouldn't be interested in her. And I don't believe he wanted her to sell off any antiques, either."

Happy swiveled around. "What do you think he was doing with Camilla?"

"That was different," Lula Mae said. "Percy wanted her to invest in a business venture. She probably would've made a bundle."

Yeah, and I saw an elephant fly past my window last night. "Any idea what kind of business venture he was starting up?" I asked.

She shrugged. "He never said anything to me about starting a business."

"Lucille has men's toiletries in her bathroom," Happy blurted out.

I stared at her. "What did you just say?"

"You heard me. She has a shaving kit and a bottle of men's cologne sitting right there on her bathroom counter."

"Why didn't you tell us that ten minutes ago?"

"Because you wouldn't stop talking." She lifted a shoulder. "Besides, I took a quick peek in the bedrooms and didn't see anybody."

"What about the closets? Did you check them out?"

"Of course, I did," she said. "I didn't see anything that didn't belong there."

I closed her door and went around to the driver's side. "Maybe we should keep an eye on Lucille. Find out where she's so anxious to go," I said as I slid inside the car.

I tooled down the street, pulled into the driveway of an empty house with a for-sale sign in front yard, and killed the engine. It didn't take long for Lucille to scuttle out to her car and head for town. We moseyed along behind her at a safe distance. She hit the bank, the grocery store, and the bakery, then headed home.

"This is getting us nowhere," Happy complained. "If Percy was staying with her, we probably scared him off. We should check out the next name on our list."

CHAPTER ELEVEN

In contrast to Lucille's old-fashioned place, Fran Parker's house was one of those ultra-modern designs, which overlooked the Gulf and was chock full of all kinds of strange curves and walls of glass.

"What a surprise," Fran said when she answered the door and found us standing there. "I haven't seen you three in ages."

"That could be because you're always gallivanting around the universe," Happy said.

Fran threw back her head and laughed. "I guess you're right." She opened the door wider and stepped aside. "Well, don't just stand there. Come on in and make yourselves at home."

Though Fran had to be in her early sixties, she didn't look a day over forty. The absence of sags and bags was mostly due to the skills of her plastic surgeon, but the fashionably thin body came from years of dieting and countless hours sweating it out in the gym. I hated to admit it, but my body wouldn't look half that good tucked into the same pair of black leggings and skimpy fuchsia top.

Fran led us to a room in back dominated by chrome and glass. As we sank down on the white, overstuffed furniture, she offered us refreshments, which we all promptly declined, having had our fill at Lucille's.

"You'll have to forgive me if I sound a bit dense today," Fran said. "I just got back from Greece and haven't quite adjusted to the time difference."

"For the life of me," Happy said, "I'll never understand what makes you want to tramp around in all those foreign countries, eating all that strange food, and putting up with all those funny customs they have."

Fran's eyes sparkled. "Honey, I go for the men. All those wonderful, delicious men."

"Speaking of men," I said, determined not to let this visit turn into another hour-long gabfest, "did you get a chance to meet Percy Moss before you left for Greece?"

"That lout." She wrinkled her nose in disgust. "Yeah, I met him. And he graciously offered to accompany me to Greece. My treat, of course."

"I'm sure you must be mistaken," Lula Mae said. "The Percy Moss I know has plenty of money. He wouldn't need to ask a woman to pay his way anywhere." She dug around in her purse and pulled out an object. "Why, just take a look at the ring he gave me."

Fran moved in for a closer look. Taking the ring from Lula Mae's hand, she held it up to the light. "Honey, if I'm not mistaken this ring's genuine one hundred per cent zirconium. And if I were you, I'd dump the guy right now, before he tries to sweet-talk you out of your life's savings."

Anger crept up Lula Mae's neck. "Percy would never give me a . . . *fake* ring."

"Don't fool yourself, hon." She handed the ring back. "The man probably has never had two pennies to rub together. He's nothing but a con man." Fran sighed. "Believe me, I know what I'm talking about."

Lula Mae stared at the ring in her hand.

"I take it Percy must have hit you up for money," I said.

"He tried," Fran replied, "but I'm no man's fool. I'm not spending my money making some poor guy's fantasies come true. The way I see it, he ought to be making my fantasies come true, not the other way around."

"So, I take it you haven't heard from him since you got back," Happy said.

"You got that right. And he'd better have the good sense to keep it that way."

"I guess you've heard about Camilla's death," I said.

"I sure did, hon." She grinned. "It couldn't have happened to a more deserving person."

"I thought you and Camilla had finally patched things up," Happy said.

Fran threw back her head and laughed. "Not in this lifetime."

Noting my puzzled look, Happy explained, "Camilla blocked Fran's membership to the country club several years ago."

"That must have made you pretty angry," Lula Mae commented.

Fran frowned. "Not angry enough to murder her, if that's what you're thinking. Besides, I wasn't home. Like I said, I just got back from Greece."

The conversation went downhill after that. We soon made our polite goodbyes and headed for the car. "Where does that leave us?" I asked.

Happy shoved a stray lock of hair back in place. "With a whole lot of nothing."

"Lucille and Fran both seemed pretty angry with Percy," I said. "Seems he'd be the more likely murder target. What would they get out of killing Camilla?"

Lula Mae seemed strangely quiet.

"What about you, Lula Mae," I asked. "What do you think?"

She folded her arms over her ample chest. "I think that Camilla must have stepped on somebody's toes. She was always good at that."

"Amen," Happy agreed.

"Whose toes?" I persisted.

She shrugged. "You just met one pair. I'm sure there are lots of others."

We were all feeling a little down, especially Lula Mae. "How about some lunch?" I offered, hoping to lift everyone's spirits. "My treat."

"I'm not very hungry," Lula Mae said.

"Nonsense." Happy made an effort to cheer up. "You've got to keep up your strength, hon."

"I suppose I could manage to eat a bite if you two are hungry."

We settled on fried chicken and mashed potato meals from one of those fast food places. Once the kid at the window handed us our order, I swung around behind the building and parked under the only tree in sight, hoping to catch some shade.

Happy scrambled out of the car and slid into the back seat beside Lula Mae. "Not bad," she said, after taking a bite of chicken. "Of course, my fried chicken is a hundred times better."

Despite her earlier words, Lula Mae only picked at her food. After a while, she gave up any pretense of eating. "You don't really believe Percy was broke, do you? He told me he sold drugs." She paused a moment, then amended, "The legal kind, I mean."

"You ever remember him making any sales calls?" Happy asked. "Seems to me he had an awful lot of free time on his hands. For somebody who has a job."

I swiveled around. "Let me see that ring again."

She slid it out of her purse and handed it to me. Now that I had time to really look at it, I had to agree with Fran. Something about the setting and mount didn't look right. "You really haven't known Percy all that long," I said gently, giving her back the ring.

Lula Mae began to wail. "How could I be so stupid?"

People in neighboring cars turned to stare at us. I decided

lunch was over. Shifting into reverse, I backed up, then threw the car into drive and peeled out of the parking lot.

CHAPTER TWELVE

The final name on our list was Stella Barnes. She lived in a small, but well-kept place on the outskirts of town. She answered our knock wearing a pink-quilted housecoat. Her dark brown hair was tousled, as if we'd caught her napping, and her blue-gray eyes looked tired. "You'll have to excuse me," she explained hoarsely. "I'm a little under the weather today."

The three of us shuffled inside and waited in the living room while she went to put on a pot of coffee. I looked around, admiring the tastefully furnished room done in cool shades of white and blue. Overhead, a ceiling fan whirred, stirring the air-conditioned air. Lula Mae and I sat facing Happy on matching sofas, a rectangular, glass coffee table between us.

When Stella returned with our coffee, her hair was neatly combed and a dab of rose-colored lipstick brightened her pale face. "I haven't seen you down at the Senior Citizens' Center lately," she said, settling down beside Happy and passing her a cup of the steaming brew.

"I don't get out as much as I used to," Happy said as she added cream and sugar. "My daughter here keeps me busy down at the Flower Patch." They spent an endless few minutes chatting about some of their friends from the Senior Center before Happy finally steered the conversation around to Percy.

I wasn't sure what kind of reaction to expect—anger, sadness maybe—but certainly not happiness. Stella's face lit up like a Christmas tree bulb. "Oh, that sweet man. Have you met him?

From the moment I first laid eyes on him, I knew we were meant for each other. And once he tasted my blueberry muffins, I had him drooling at my feet, begging for more."

Lula Mae frowned. "I find that hard to believe."

Stella seemed taken aback by the vehemence in her voice. "In fact, Percy loves my muffins so much," she went on, though less enthusiastically, "we've decided to open a bakery together."

Alarmed by where she seemed to be heading, I blurted out, "I hope you didn't give him any money."

Stella looked at me, downright puzzled. "Why, sure I did, hon. Like I said, we're planning on opening a business together. The man was a financial genius. He found us this great deal on some used equipment, only five thousand dollars. But we had to move fast, or . . ." Her words trailed off when she noticed Happy's worried expression.

"Is something wrong?" she asked. "Has something happened to Percy? If it has, don't be afraid to tell me. I'm a lot stronger than I look."

Happy sat down her cup and saucer. "By now you must've heard about Camilla Davenport's murder."

"Sure I have," Stella replied. "I didn't know her all that well, but no one deserves to die like that—murdered right in her own home. But I don't understand what that's got to do with Percy's bakery."

"The police seemed to feel," Happy said, "that Percy had something to do with Camilla's death."

What little color there was in Stella's face disappeared, giving her a ghostlike appearance. "Why would they think that?" she asked, her words barely audible.

"For one thing," I said, "he was having dinner with her the night she was killed."

"There's no law against that." Even though she defended his

actions, Stella seemed more than a little shaken by the revelation.

Finally, Lula Mae could take no more. Springing to her feet, she said, "But the police are wrong. My fiancé—ex-fiancé," she corrected, "might be a thief, but he would never murder anyone."

"What do you mean *your* fiancé?" The life was suddenly back in Stella's face. "The man happens to be *my* fiancé." And to prove her point she reached into the pocket of her housecoat and dug out a ring. A ring identical to the one tucked away in Lula Mae's purse.

"What did the man do?" I blurted out before thinking. "Buy the things wholesale?"

Lula Mae cast a withering glance in my direction, then stormed out of the room. Anxious to make amends, I leaped up and went after her, leaving Happy to deal with Percy's second, or was that first, fiancée.

"You just wait until I get my hands on that man," Lula Mae said as she paced back and forth next to the car. "Why, I'll . . . I'll . . . murder him myself."

Happy came striding down the walkway. "Then I suggest you get in line." She nodded toward the house. "You aren't the only woman eager for a piece of that man's hide."

CHAPTER THIRTEEN

We were a subdued bunch as we headed back to Bessie's to retrieve my truck. But not so subdued that the aroma of barbecue didn't lure us inside. We ordered drinks, then placed an order for three roast beef sandwiches to go. While we were waiting for our order, I headed for the phone to call Jolene.

"How are things going?" I asked when she picked up.

"We've been super busy. Hold on." She paused to count out change, then she was back. "You'll be happy to know we've sold off most of those sour kumquats you were so worried about. As a matter of fact," she sounded proud of herself, "I managed to unload six other citrus trees."

"Any problems you can't handle?"

"Not really. But don't forget I have to be out of here by five. I have a date this evening and I need at least a couple of hours to get ready."

"That's no problem. I'll be back as soon as I finish my soda. That should give you plenty of time to get ready for this dream man."

"For your information," she informed me, "he is a dream man. Smart, handsome, and best of all—loaded."

"He sounds too good to be true."

"There you go again—being negative. How many times am I going to have to tell you: if you want good things to happen, you have to think positive thoughts?"

"Yeah, yeah. You've told me that a million times already. I get the idea."

I was on the verge of hanging up when I heard her call out, "I almost forgot. Some cop came by looking for you."

My stomach tightened. "Lieutenant Griggs?"

"Yeah, I think that was his name."

An interval of silence passed. Finally, I asked, "Did he mention what he wanted?"

"No. But he left a number." There was a brief pause while she rooted around for it. "Here it is." As she read off the number, I grabbed a pen off a passing waitress and jotted it down on a pilfered napkin.

I hung up the phone, dug around in my purse for more change, then dialed the number she'd given me. "Were you looking for me?" I asked, when Steven finally came on the line.

"I can't believe you don't have a cell phone," he said. "Or was Jolene just feeding me a line?"

"No, I don't have a cell phone. Don't want one. Have no intention of getting one."

"Everybody has one."

"Not me," I said. "Now, did you have a purpose for getting in touch with me, or should I get back to what I was doing?"

"I was hoping you might know where Lula Mae is. I've been by her place several times, but she hasn't been around."

"As a matter of fact," I said, "she's here with me. Why are you looking for her? Have you found Percy? Have you figured out who murdered Camilla?"

He ignored my questions. "Where's here?"

"Bessie's Kitchen." I tried not to let the irritation I felt creep into my voice.

"What's she doing there?"

"Same as you'd like to be doing," I said. "Having a glass of iced tea. Enjoying the sweet smell of barbecue."

I thought I heard a chuckle.

"Do you know if she's heard from Percy?"

He was really starting to annoy me. "No, she hasn't heard from Percy. And if she had, I don't think she'd be inclined to tell you."

Switching to his cop voice, he asked, "Are you implying that she'd withhold evidence from the police?"

"I'm not saying that at all," I backpedaled. "What I meant was—"

"Never mind," he said, letting me off the hook. "Before she turns on the news tonight, you might want to let her know that we've located Percy's car. It was out by the lake. The keys were left in the ignition."

I took a moment to process the information. "That doesn't make any sense."

"Since some nitwit already leaked it to the press, you can also tell her we recovered a diamond necklace. It was hidden under the front seat, wrapped in a man's handkerchief."

"You're thinking it belonged to Camilla?"

"Seems likely. We haven't had any other reports of stolen jewelry. I'm headed over to the motel now to see if her son can identify it."

"Motel?"

"In case you've forgotten," he explained, "the house is still a crime scene."

My conscience nudged me to tell him about the money Percy had taken from Stella to buy bakery equipment, but I conveniently ignored it and threw out another question. "Why would Percy abandon his car out by the lake and leave a diamond necklace under the seat that might link him to a murder? Nobody could be that stupid."

"You'd be surprised by how stupid some of these guys are."

"It seems to me, if Percy had killed Camilla, he'd be halfway

81

to Mexico by now. Without wheels, how's he planning on getting out of town?"

"You're beginning to think like a cop."

I ignored him. "Any reports of cars missing in the area?"

"Nope."

"Then how—"

"Maybe Percy didn't leave the car behind voluntarily," he cut in.

"You're not implying something has happened to Percy, are you?"

"Forget I said anything," he said, a little too quickly.

"If you know something that you're not telling me . . ." I deliberately let the sentence trail off, hoping he'd feel compelled to offer more.

I heard someone call to him in the background. "Look," he said briskly, "I have to go. Don't worry about Percy. I'm sure he'll turn up soon."

When I got back to the table, Happy and Lula Mae were having themselves a good old time discussing all the things they planned to do to Percy once they found him. But instead of relishing the latest news I related to them, their faces clouded in dismay.

"What's the matter?" I asked. "A minute ago you two were ready to roast the man alive."

"Oh, that," Happy said. "We were just blowing off a little steam. We didn't really mean anything by it. In case you haven't noticed, we're not criminals."

"Then maybe you shouldn't go around threatening to murder the man in public," I suggested, "or somebody might get the wrong idea."

"You just don't understand." Lula Mae began to sniffle. "I thought Percy really loved me. I thought we were going to spend the rest of our lives together. Now I find out—" She broke off, unable to continue. Snatching up her napkin, she began to dab at her eyes. A moment later, she hoisted her large frame from the chair and waddled off toward the ladies' room.

I sighed. "You'd better go after her."

Happy made no move to follow Lula Mae. "She'll probably be in there a while."

I glanced at my watch. "She'd better not be in there too long. I've got to relieve Jolene at the Flower Patch soon. She has a big date."

Happy didn't seem to be listening. "We have no choice," she finally said, her gaze fastening on me. "We've got to find Percy and clear his name. Otherwise, Lula Mae will always be known as the woman who was engaged to that murderer."

I thought she was going a little too far, but yeah, I knew this wasn't something we could walk away from. Not with Lula Mae's reputation on the line. Not to mention, her emotional well being.

CHAPTER FOURTEEN

By the time Happy returned from the bathroom with Lula Mae, the ice had melted in their drinks. They didn't seem all that thirsty anyway. Bessie handed them the bag with our sandwiches, and they headed home.

I, on the other hand, headed for the Flower Patch to relieve Jolene. Heaven forbid she wouldn't have oodles of time to get ready for her big date. The moment she caught sight of me, she gathered up her things and flew out the door. I shook my head. "He must be some guy."

Business began to taper off about half an hour before closing time. By then, I was so worn out I didn't mind the idea of losing a sale or two. I closed out the register and headed outside to lock the gate, which was something my dear mother often forgot to do, having been raised in an era when people weren't afraid to leave their doors unlocked.

Before I could get the padlock on, Steven zipped into the parking lot. He grinned, then climbed out of his squad car and moseyed through the gate as if he owned the place. "Care to join me?" Without waiting for a reply, he headed toward the nearest bench and plopped down.

After snapping the padlock in place to prevent any more last-minute shoppers, I trailed after him and plunked my tired body down on the opposite end of the bench he was occupying, as far away from him as I could get without falling off.

The sweet smell of gardenias perfumed the still warm air.

Sunlight filtering through an oak tree overhead dappled our skin. I wanted to relax and enjoy the moment, but I could feel him studying me. Squirming about, I tried to get comfortable. Finally, I blurted out, "What is it? Do I have dirt plastered across my face or something?"

"No." A slow grin spread from his mouth and settled in his soft, gray eyes. "I was just taking a moment to enjoy the scenery."

My pulse quickened. A feeling of intense pleasure battled with an equally intense need for escape. The warring factions drove me to my feet. Marching over to a display of concrete statues, I stood with my back to him. "Since you're so interested in the scenery, I'm sure you'll want to check out our collection of garden accessories. They add that special touch to the landscape that so many people are looking for these days."

He stepped up behind me, so close his breath tickled the back of my neck. "Is that so?"

A shiver of excitement swept through me, along with a rising sense of panic. This wouldn't do. This wouldn't do at all.

Forcing my body into action, I shot over to a particularly large specimen and began to recite its unique features. At least, that's what I hoped was spilling out of my mouth. The circuits in my brain seemed to be temporarily without power.

He trailed after me with that stupid grin on his face. "Are you afraid of me?"

"Certainly not."

"Then why do you keep running away from me?"

Squaring my body into a don't-mess-with-me stance, I said, "I don't run from anybody."

"Then what was that business about Atlanta?"

Some of the starch went out of my stance. "That was different."

"How so?"

I leaned down to right a concrete angel, which had toppled

85

over. "It just was."

His eyes narrowed. "You can do better than that."

My chin jutted out stubbornly.

When he realized I had no intention of answering, he went on, "If you didn't want to get married—"

"I never said that."

The cop in him pushed for answers. "So you did want to marry me?"

As if the air was suddenly devoid of oxygen, I began to suck in quick gulps of air.

Realizing what was happening, he reached over and took my hand. "You're hyperventilating. You need to breathe slowly. In and out. That's it." He continued his coaching until my breathing returned to normal.

"Feel better now?" he asked.

I nodded. We stood there a moment, gazes locked, then the power clicked back on in my brain and I seized on an idea that was sure to shift his attention away from the past. "Did you know Percy had a lot of cash on him the night he disappeared?"

"Is that so?" He seemed thrown off balance for a moment, but managed to recover quickly, sliding behind that police shield he wore so well. "Exactly how did you come across that information?"

Too late I realized my mistake. "Because . . ." I had no choice, but to tell him about Percy's less-than-honorable intentions toward the three women we'd interviewed, and the five thousand dollars he'd taken from Stella.

"Sounds as if the guy was a regular Romeo," he said when I'd finished.

"Seems that way. But what I don't get is, why is he still walking around free instead of buried in some prison cell where he'll never see the light of day?"

"Probably because none of the women involved wanted to

86

step forward and admit they'd been conned."

I saw his point. "You said Percy's car was found out by the lake. There are lots of cabins out that way. You don't suppose he's holed up in one?"

"So far we haven't found anyone who's seen him."

"Probably because no one wants to talk to the police. But they might be more receptive to a local business owner trying to find a missing relative."

"You stay out of this," he said firmly.

The frown on my face must have told him what I thought of his suggestion.

Realizing he'd taken the wrong approach, his voice softened. "Look, maybe you don't understand how serious this situation is. There's a killer out there somewhere, and I don't want you becoming his next victim."

"Of all the chauvinistic, pigheaded ideas."

"Hey," he held up a hand, "I'm just trying to look out for you."

"For your information, I don't need you to look after me."

He seemed annoyed. "Why don't you just stick to your plants and leave the police work to us? That's what we get paid for."

"In case you haven't noticed," I said, squaring my shoulders, "your police force can't even find one old man."

"We'll find him soon enough. Don't you worry." He paused a moment, then added, "What we don't need is for a bunch of civilians to put themselves in danger, so we have to spend all our time worrying about them, instead of chasing down leads."

"Leads like"—I lifted my brows—"the women Percy conned money out of?"

He brushed aside my comment. "There's also the little matter of chain of evidence we cops have to concern ourselves with."

"It's not like I'm planning on becoming a vigilante."

A wall of steel slid down over his face. "Katie, for once in your life, do the smart thing and trust somebody besides yourself."

CHAPTER FIFTEEN

The next morning, I drove out to the lake and spent several hours canvassing the area. In the end, I had no better luck than the police. Tired and itching from a passel of mosquito bites, I finally gave up and went home.

Trouble waited for me on the front porch. As soon as I turned into the driveway, Happy flew down the steps. Her face was tense with worry. "Thank goodness, you're back."

Before I had a chance to ask her what was wrong, she heaved the door to my truck open and climbed inside. "Quick, we've got to get down to police headquarters right away. They've hauled Lula Mae in for questioning."

"That's ridiculous!" I said, when it finally dawned on me she wasn't kidding. "What in the world possessed them to do such a thing?"

She urged me to get moving. "We can talk on the way."

As we sped toward the police station, I tried to pry more information out of her. But she only hemmed and hawed and skirted around the facts. Only when I threatened to turn the truck around and head back home did she break down and admit, "Someone may have seen Lula Mae at Camilla's house the night she was murdered."

"What?" I veered to the side of the road and parked. My hands trembled from suppressed anger, or fear; I'm not sure which. Gathering what shreds of patience I could muster, I turned to her and said, "Start at the beginning and don't leave anything out. Not the single, most minute detail."

"There's not much to tell."

"Start with how Lula Mae got to Camilla's in the first place. Did she take a taxi? Get a ride with a neighbor? Fly over there?"

She gave me a haughty stare when I tossed out that last suggestion.

I returned it.

She was the first to crack. "I reckon she was more upset than I figured. After you drove her home, I suppose she got to thinking about Camilla and Percy being alone in that big old house."

I knew from years of experience it would do no good to rush her, so I nodded and let her ramble on.

"Well, I'm sure you can imagine the ideas that went through her head." She shuddered. "So instead of sitting there stewing all night, Lula Mae revved up George's old Cadillac and whipped over there, intent on giving the two of them a piece of her mind."

"Wait a minute." I held up a hand. "Correct me if I'm wrong, but Lula Mae doesn't know how to drive."

"It's true Lula Mae doesn't have a driver's license. But when she has to, she can usually manage to get where she's going. Especially if she takes her time. The problem is, she tends to run into things. That's how come George would never let her drive."

I gave her a hard stare. "You're telling me that Lula Mae drove herself over to Camilla's?"

Happy nodded. "I'm surprised that old clunker even cranked. She told me she was so nervous being behind the wheel again that she nearly ran into the light pole backing out. But once she got on the road, she did all right."

"You knew about all this?"

Avoiding my eyes, she nodded.

I could feel my temper start to rise. "And you didn't try to stop her?"

Happy folded her arms across her chest. "I didn't know about it until later. Besides, she's a grown woman, not some two-year-old child that I can order around."

Like that didn't happen all the time.

"Okay." I moved on. "So what happened when she got to Camilla's?"

"Nothing earth-shattering. She marched inside, gave Camilla a good chewing out, then went home and had a good cry."

Hope began to rise. "So Camilla was still alive when she left?"

Happy glared at me as if she couldn't believe I would ask such a question. "Of course."

"Did this happen before or after Percy's visit?"

"After . . . no . . . before." She frowned, as if annoyed by the question. "How should I know?"

"You're the one with the inside scoop."

Her backbone stiffened. "For your information, Lula Mae doesn't tell me everything."

With a sigh, I cranked up the engine and pulled back into traffic. "Well, I hope she realizes how much trouble she's gotten herself into. She should never have gone over to Camilla's. What was she thinking?"

Wisely, Happy didn't answer.

When we arrived at police headquarters, it was to face even graver news: an anonymous tip had led the police to search George's car. A velvet case was found under the front seat containing a pair of diamond earrings, which matched the necklace found in Percy's car. Naturally, Lula Mae denied having any knowledge of how the earrings got there.

I glared at Steven. "What were you doing searching Uncle George's car without a warrant in the first place?"

"Didn't need it. Lula Mae gave us permission to search the vehicle."

"Of course, she did," Happy said, building up a head of steam. "Doesn't that tell you something?"

"Look, Mrs. Spencer, I have to investigate every leads that comes into this office," Steven said in that calm, even, cop voice. "Otherwise, I wouldn't be doing my job."

"Hog wash." Happy squared her shoulders. "I demand to see my sister at once."

Steven pointed. "She's down the hall. I was getting ready to drive her home myself."

He led us to a narrow room filled with three small tables, a pair of vending machines, and a rectangular table holding a half-empty pot of coffee. Hunkered down in a metal chair at the nearest table sat Lula Mae, looking forlorn, her purse clutched protectively over her abdomen.

Happy rushed over and gave her shoulder a pat. "Don't worry, dear, we've come to rescue you. This young man had no right to drag you off to this . . . place. Unfortunately, he still has a lot to learn about respecting his elders." After giving Steven the evil eye, she ushered Lula Mae from the room, murmuring words of comfort.

As I started after them, Steven grabbed my arm. "I suggest you take your aunt home and give her a sedative. She's wound up tighter than one of those old wind-up alarm clocks."

"What? You thought you'd drag her down here, bombard her with questions, and she'd be dancing with glee?"

"She came with me willingly," he pointed out. "Besides, how was I supposed to get anything out of her with your mother answering every question for her?"

He had a valid point. Happy's bulldog qualities sprang to life whenever one of her family members was threatened. "I hope you're satisfied that Lula Mae is the innocent victim in all this."

He shrugged. "We're not charging her with anything at this time."

The man was really getting on my nerves. "Has it occurred to you that this anonymous caller is probably your killer? That he, or she, is trying to frame Lula Mae for something she didn't do?"

He let out a noisy breath. "Give me some credit. I've been doing this a long time."

Was that a yes or a no? I decided to go with the former. "Okay, then." I headed for the door.

Before I could get far, he called out, "Could you do me a favor?"

I turned around and eyed him with suspicion.

"Would you tell Lula Mae not to leave town. We'll probably need to talk to her again."

I snatched back all the brownie points I'd given him for not being an imbecile. Following Happy's example, I gave him the evil eye, then marched out of the room with my head held high, before I did something I'd seriously regret.

CHAPTER SIXTEEN

Outside the station, Happy and Lula Mae waited for me on the sidewalk. As I hurried over to join them, Lula Mae's chest swelled up and words began to explode from her mouth. "That Lieutenant Griggs of yours seems to think I was jealous of Percy's relationship with Camilla. When I explained that there was no relationship, and that Percy only wanted to borrow money from Camilla, not marry her, he got all huffy with me."

I decided not to cloud the issue by reminding her that Percy had already asked two women to marry him. That we knew about.

Still on a roll, Lula Mae went on, "The nerve of that man. I'm surprised he didn't lock me up with all the other riffraff in that place."

"I know, dear," Happy said soothingly, "it must've been just awful for you."

"It was!" Lula Mae's voice ratcheted up a notch. "Why, the man treated me like some . . . some common criminal."

If you asked me, the police had good reason to treat her like a common criminal. She had means: she could wallop someone over the head as well as anyone. She had motive: Camilla was out to steal her fiancé. And she also had opportunity: thanks to this anonymous source who'd placed her at the scene near the time of the murder. When you add in the earrings found in Uncle's George's car, even I had to wonder about her innocence.

"Where did those earrings come from?" I demanded.

Lula Mae's face turned fire-engine red. Flames of anger shot from her eyes. Though my knees trembled, I screwed up my courage and said, "Well?"

Seconds ticked by. Finally, she twisted her head up huffily and said, "I found those earrings outside my front door the day after Camilla passed on. They were wrapped in wedding paper. Pardon me if I thought they were a gift from Percy."

I rolled my eyes, wondering how she could be so gullible. "Uh-huh."

Lula Mae caught the skepticism in my voice. "It was not unusual for Percy to give me little presents now and then," she said in her defense.

"When he was on the run for murder?"

Happy stepped in front of Lula Mae and cast the evil eye in my direction. "That's enough, young lady."

"It's all right, Happy." Lula Mae gently nudged her aside. "We might as well get this over with so our baby girl can quit worrying."

With obvious reluctance, Happy gave in, and motioned for Lula Mae to continue with her explanation.

"Like I was saying," Lula Mae said, "Percy gave me little presents now and then. He was sweet like that. Only this time, I was just so furious with him that I threw his gift into the trashcan out back. I figured the earrings were probably fakes anyway. Like the ring he gave me."

Made sense, in a woman-scorned, getting-even, kind of way. "Then how did they get under the front seat of Uncle George's car?"

She shrugged. "I have no idea."

"Oh, for goodness sakes," Happy said. "Everybody knows Lula Mae never locks that stupid old car. Who in their right mind would want to steal it? It's almost fifteen years old. The killer saw an opportunity to frame Lula Mae, and took it."

"That's right." Lula Mae folded her arms across her ample bosom and glared at me. "The killer stuck them under the seat of George's car to frame me. I'm perfectly innocent."

Somehow I had to make Lula Mae understand the seriousness of her situation. "You're in deep trouble here. A woman that *you* were not on the best of terms with has been robbed and murdered. The man *you* were engaged to has been two-timing you with the murder victim, and has most likely skipped town. And if that's not enough to nail the lid on your coffin, here *you* are, in possession of a pair of earrings belonging to the deceased."

"Lula Mae's done nothing wrong." Happy rushed to her sister's defense. "Except put her trust in the wrong man. We don't even know for certain those earrings belonged to Camilla. For all we know, Percy could've bought them ages ago."

I scowled at her. "You know as well as I do that—"

"I don't know any such thing," Happy said with a note of finality. "And even if Percy did steal the earrings from Camilla, Lula Mae didn't have anything to do with it."

"Yeah." Lula Mae got into the act. "The only thing I did was throw them in the trash."

"Then someone is going to an awful lot of trouble to make you look guilty," I said.

"Probably that pea-brained Percy," Happy said. "He's the one who dragged her into this mess in the first place."

"Follow the money. That's what all those TV detectives say," Lula Mae told us. "So my guess is, one of Camilla's kids knocked her off to get at their inheritance."

"Sounds reasonable to me," Happy said, putting an end to our discussion. "Now, if you don't mind, I'd like to get my baby sister home. Your young man has put her through quite enough for one day."

"How many times am I going to have to say this? Steven is not my young man."

Ignoring me, Happy slipped an arm around Lula Mae's shoulders and led her toward the truck. Watching them, I felt this ache deep in my gut. "Whatever possessed you to go over to Camilla's in the first place?" I called out.

The twosome came to an abrupt stop and turned around in unison. Happy took it upon herself to enlighten me. "Camilla was out to steal Percy from Lula Mae."

Good riddance, I started to say, but the misery in Lula Mae's eyes stopped me. "Did you mention anything about your wedding plans to Camilla?"

"I told her, all right," Lula Mae said. "The heifer laughed in my face and told me I wasn't the kind of woman who could hang on to a man like Percy for long. That she'd be there when he came to his senses."

I felt like a monster for bringing up the subject. "I'm sure she was just trying to get back at you for stealing Uncle George from her."

"Uncle George was never *hers* in the first place." Happy set me straight.

"Yeah, well. Whatever." I circled around to the driver's side and crawled inside.

Lula Mae and Happy scooted in next to me. "Now," Happy told Lula Mae, "you just put this whole traumatic incident out of your mind. Until Camilla's killer is behind bars, you're coming home with us." Happy leaned forward trying to catch my eye.

Wasn't she practically living with us already?

"She's right, Lula Mae." I picked up my cue. "There's no way we'd let you stay in that big old house alone. At a time like this, you belong with family."

Having earned my brownie points for the day, I settled back

and only half listened as Lula Mae launched into a detailed description of the inquisition the police had put her through. The way she told it, she'd endured something straight out of the Middle Ages.

After a while, I tuned them out. All those phone calls on Percy's bill began to nag at me. Maybe they were worth checking into. Besides—I glanced toward the twosome sitting beside me—I'd had about all the togetherness I could handle for one day.

CHAPTER SEVENTEEN

The instant we arrived home, Happy whisked Lula Mae up to the guest room and got her settled. Seizing the opportunity, I rooted around in my purse for the paper where I'd scribbled down the number on Percy's bill. After checking to be sure Happy wasn't lurking about, I made a dash for the phone.

The ringing on the other end seemed to go on forever. I was on the verge of hanging up when someone finally picked up. "Mulberry's," a deep male voice informed me, "the special today is meatloaf, mashed potatoes and gravy, and green beans."

After jotting down the address, I slammed down the phone and grabbed my keys. With only a smidgen of guilt, I pilfered a snapshot of Percy out of Lula Mae's purse, which she had conveniently left on the hall table. "I'm off to take care of some errands," I yelled up the stairs, then shot out of there before Happy had time to question me.

It took nearly an hour to reach my destination—a cheap diner in an older section of town, crowded between a hardware store and a shoe shop. Inside, the place was crammed with bright orange tables. Weaving my way through the crowd of mostly working-class men, I snagged the only available space near the end of the counter.

"Busy place," I remarked to the chunky waitress with frizzy brown hair who took my order for a cheeseburger and fries.

"Tell me about it." She shoved a glass of iced tea in my direction. "Most of these guys work second shift down at the docks."

Someone at the opposite end of the counter yelled for more coffee. "I ain't deaf," she grumbled as she snatched up the coffeepot and headed over to refill his cup.

I was forced to nurse a piece of pecan pie and two more cups of coffee before the place emptied enough to engage the overworked waitress in more conversation. "I was wondering if you might be able to help me." I shoved the snapshot I'd taken from Lula Mae's purse toward her. "I'm looking for my uncle." My conscience prodded me to clarify the uncle part, but I figured Percy had come close enough to being my uncle that most folks would say we were practically kin. "I thought you might have seen him around."

The waitress took a quick glance at the picture, then handed it back. "Yeah, I've seen him. He used to come in here all the time." She wiped up a spill on the counter. "He ain't been around lately though."

"The thing is," I said, "he was supposed to show up at a wedding, but nobody's heard from him. I thought I'd better find out if he's okay, before my mama sends the posse out looking for him."

"Say no more. I got a mama too." She scooted over to the window, which separated the dining area from the kitchen, and yelled at somebody named Jonah. A second later, a beefy guy with a crew cut shuffled up to the opening.

"There a problem here?" he asked.

"Remember that fellow who used to come in here all the time, the one who sat over by the window with his nose glued to the paper?"

"Yeah, what about him?"

"This here's his niece." She nodded in my direction. "Seems he didn't show up for some wedding, so her mama sent her down here to check on him."

"I didn't know he had any family." Jonah disappeared from

sight, only to reappear moments later in the dining room. Wiping his hands on a big, checkered dishtowel, he lumbered toward me. "You might want to check with Mrs. Mayfield; she's probably heard from him."

"Mrs. Mayfield?" Another victim?

He took a moment before answering. "Look, I don't know how well you know your uncle . . ." His eyes sought mine.

Hoping to put him at ease, I said, "Let's just say, nothing he does would surprise me."

He started to reply, when a short, skinny guy in blue denim work pants slid onto the stool beside me. Jonah motioned me to a table in the corner where we could talk more privately.

"Sometimes when things got slow around here, I'd come out and grab a cup of coffee with your uncle. He seemed to enjoy the company." Jonah shifted around in his chair, as if he couldn't get comfortable. "Anyway, like Betty Ann said, he always had his nose glued to the newspaper."

So far he hadn't given me anything to work with. "Lots of people like to read the paper when they're eating alone. I do it myself all the time."

"Yeah, but I bet you don't spend all your time pouring over the obituaries."

He had me there. "If I were his age and wanted to keep up with old friends who might have passed away, I might."

He wouldn't meet my eyes. Always a bad sign. "His main interest seemed to be in finding lonely widows in need of a strong shoulder to lean on."

I shook my head, not really surprised by what I was hearing. "I can't believe any woman in her right mind would fall for that."

"That's just it," he said. "Most of them are so overwhelmed with grief, they aren't thinking too clearly. For many of them it's the first time they've been alone in maybe forty or fifty years. They're scared. And when some guy comes along offering to take care of them—"

"They jump at the chance," I finished his thought. Interesting, but it didn't explain all those phone calls on Percy's bill. "Betty Ann said she hadn't seen my uncle around lately. How about you?"

"Nope, but Mrs. Mayfield probably has."

"Who is this Mrs. Mayfield you keep talking about, and what does she have to do with my uncle?"

He smiled sheepishly. "She owns this place. She and your uncle used to be pretty tight."

"I take it she's a widow."

He nodded.

"So my uncle and this Mrs. Mayfield are . . ." I sought for the correct word and came up with, "an item. You'd think he'd be around more."

"The thing is, one minute they're madly in love, and the next minute, they're fighting like cats and dogs."

"But it's over now?" I wanted to be clear.

He looked thoughtful. "Now that you mention it, I think they're in one of their at-each-other's-throat phases."

Curiosity got the best of me. "Any idea why?"

"I think it had something to do with that hare-brained idea he had about opening a bakery. Let's face it, if the man can't boil water, how's he going to bake muffins?"

"You have a good point."

"Tell that to Mrs. Mayfield."

Alarm bells went off in my head. "She hasn't given him any money, I hope."

He shrugged. "She asked for my opinion about this bakery idea of his. I gave it to her. Whether she listened, or not, I have no idea."

"Maybe if you told her about this obituary business."

"It wouldn't do any good," he said with regret. "She's convinced he really cares about her."

My mind came back to all those phone calls on Percy's statement. "Is Mrs. Mayfield in here a lot?"

"Not so much since her husband passed on."

"That's strange. Because Uncle Percy seems to call this place quite a lot. I thought he must be talking to Mrs. Mayfield, but if she's not in here that often . . ." I let the sentence hang.

"Your uncle hasn't been calling Mrs. Mayfield," he told me. "He's been calling me. He wants me to make Mrs. Mayfield an offer on this place."

Alarm bells ratcheted up a notch. "Does she want to sell this place?"

"She's never said anything to me about it. But if your uncle has anything to say about it, she will."

He didn't need to say any more. I had firsthand knowledge of how women acted once they got caught in Percy's web of lies.

We sat there a minute in silence. Jonah seemed relieved when the frizzy-headed waitress clipped an order to the carousel and spun it toward the kitchen. He nodded to let her know he saw the order, then pushed himself up and wished me luck finding my uncle.

Before he could slip away, I asked him for directions to Mrs. Mayfield's house.

CHAPTER EIGHTEEN

After backtracking to correct a few wrong turns, I eased to a stop before a small, but neatly kept, house of early 1950s vintage. It was painted a soft shade of green. A couple of oversized, white rockers sat invitingly on the porch, which ran across the entire width of the house.

I sprinted up concrete steps and rang the doorbell. A few minutes later, the porch light winked on. A face appeared in the beveled window in the center of the door. It disappeared, and the door creaked open a few seconds later, as far as the safety chain allowed.

"Can I help you?" The voice was high-pitched, almost squeaky.

"Hi. I'm Kate Spencer. I'm looking for my uncle, Percy Moss. Jonah down at the diner told me you might know where he is."

The door closed and reopened, minus the chain. "I don't recall Percy mentioning any niece." Caramel-brown eyes studied my face.

"What uncle wants to admit to having a niece old enough to vote?"

A smile lit her face. "I can certainly understand the feeling. When you get to be my age, you don't exactly look forward to birthdays."

As she ushered me inside, I found myself liking this slender woman with her mop of curly, brown hair. "Make yourself at home." She pointed toward a brown sofa, its arms and back covered with crocheted doilies. "I'll put us on a pot of tea."

"Please don't go to any trouble."

"No trouble," she replied, sauntering off.

I looked around. The place reminded me of Grandma Rose's house, all cozy and warm and cluttered with knickknacks.

Mrs. Mayfield soon returned, carrying a large, silver tray. She placed it on the polished oak coffee table, then handed me one of the dainty, pink-flowered cups. "How about a gingersnap cookie? Made them myself this morning." She grinned and sat down beside me. "They were my late husband's favorite."

I took a sip of tea, some kind of herbal blend, and got down to business. "Jonah said that you and my uncle are good friends."

"Oh, my, yes." Her eyes sparkled. "Percy and I are the best of friends. He's such a dear man. Well, most of the time anyway," she amended.

How did the guy do it? Get all these women to believe he was so wonderful?

"If you don't mind my asking, how did you and my uncle meet?"

A flicker of pain crossed her face. "I'm afraid we met under rather unfortunate circumstances. Last year when my Lester passed away, your uncle was kind enough to attend his funeral."

A sickening jolt of anger swept through me. I wanted to shout: Louse. Double louse. But, of course, I didn't.

Noting my fierce expression, she hurried to explain, "It turns out, Percy and my husband served in Vietnam together."

"Do you remember your husband ever mentioning him?"

"Well, no. I don't remember him saying anything about Percy, but then, Lester never wanted to talk about his experiences during that horrible period of his life."

My guess was, Percy had never set foot in Vietnam. "When Percy heard about Lester's death," Mrs. Mayfield went on, "he felt it was his duty to make sure I was taken care of. The two of them being such good buddies and all."

"That must have been a comfort." I longed to tell her about all the other women Percy was "taking care of." But I didn't have the heart to spoil her illusion.

She leaned forward to pat my hand. "A blessing from heaven, that's what your uncle's been to me."

It was all I could do to sit still.

"He was a tremendous help sorting through Lester's papers. The truth is, I don't think I would've made it through those days without him."

"Uncle Percy is a real whiz with paperwork. In fact, he's been talking about starting his own business."

She seemed surprised. "You know about the bakery?"

I nodded.

"It's just," she said, looking confused, "Percy asked me not to mention it to anyone. At least, not until he had all the financing in place."

"But Jonah—"

"Oh, Jonah." She batted a hand in the air. "He's family."

"How does he feel about you investing in a bakery?"

She set down her cup. "To tell you the truth, he doesn't much like the idea."

"Sounds like a wise man."

"Of course, he's probably afraid I might sell the diner so I could help Percy open The Muffin House. That's what your uncle planned to call his place."

"Which you'd never do." I wanted to hear her say the words.

"Certainly not." She seemed appalled by the idea. "The diner was Lester's baby. I would never think of selling the place. At least, not until I get so decrepit I can't take care of myself anymore. Lester always said—"

"When was the last time you heard from Percy?" I said, before she could get off on a tangent about her late husband.

"Let me think." She pursed her lips. "Probably not for a month, at least. He had some business matters to wrap up in Georgia—resigning his job, selling his house, that sort of stuff."

I breathed a sigh of relief. "So you haven't given him any money to buy equipment, or anything?"

"Well . . ." she hesitated. "There was this deal he found on an oven. He had to act fast. Before someone else snatched it up."

I bit back a groan. "How much?"

"Promise you won't tell Jonah?"

"Cross my heart, hope to die," I said.

"I managed to scrape together five thousand dollars." She spoke so softly, I had to lean forward to hear her.

I didn't have the heart to tell her there would be no bakery. Or about the other partner who'd already given Percy five thousand dollars for a nonexistent oven.

I dug around in my purse for a business card. Flipping it over, I jotted down my home number and handed it to her. "If you hear from Percy, please give me a call."

A new thought seemed to occur to her. "Percy's not in any trouble is he?"

"Nothing to worry about," I assured her. "Uncle Percy tends to disappear from time to time, but he always shows up sooner or later."

The furrows between her brows vanished. "Thank goodness. For a minute there I thought—"

"There's no need to worry," I hurried to assure her.

"You'll let me know if you hear from him before I do," she said. "He may get on my nerves sometimes, but I really do care about him."

"Of course."

Before I left, she pressed a plastic container filled with gingersnap cookies into my hand. I thanked her for the cookies and promised to visit again soon.

CHAPTER NINETEEN

Community Fellowship church was jammed with family, friends, and acquaintances eager to pay their respects to Camilla Davenport. Happy, Lula Mae, and I managed to snag a seat near the front.

Promptly at ten o'clock, Reverend Cobb slid behind the podium and began to extol the virtues of the dearly departed. I soon found my thoughts drifting to other matters. Such as why those earrings had turned up on Lula Mae's front porch. And, more importantly, who had put them there? For I was absolutely certain of one thing—Lula Mae was telling the truth about having found them on her doorstep.

But what if the robbery was only a smokescreen? Which led to the obvious question: Who wanted Camilla dead? And why?

I glanced around at the solemn faces surrounding me. Could a cold-blooded killer be hiding among them, wearing the mask of a friend?

A shiver worked its way up my spine that had nothing to do with the temperature inside the church. Surely, there had to be some other explanation. An outsider—maybe a rich widow, who'd been conned out of her life savings—wanted to get even with Percy. Only Camilla had somehow gotten in the way.

Thankfully, the service drew to a close, and I was able to push aside all those useless speculations. Along with the other mourners, I filed outside, climbed into my vehicle, and followed the hearse to the cemetery, where we endured another lengthy discourse on the good doings of the dearly departed. When the Reverend's words finally dried up, we trudged to our cars en masse and trailed the family back to Camilla's.

Well, most of us trailed the family back to Camilla's. It came as no surprise that Happy and Lula Mae decided to bow out. But not me. I marched inside, stacked my plate up with all sorts of goodies, then wandered around listening to all the chatter taking place. Who knew? I might get lucky and stumble across some tidbit of information that would point me in the direction of Camilla's killer and restore Lula Mae's good name.

In my wanderings, I bumped into Steven, who was huddled near the refreshment table. I almost didn't recognize him in a navy suit and blue silk tie. Like me, his plate was piled high with a vast assortment of goodies.

"What are you doing here?" I demanded.

He took a bite of some strawberry, whipped cream stuff. "Same thing you're doing here—paying my respects to the family and enjoying all the good food."

I opened my mouth to set him straight. I wasn't here just to pay my respects; I was also here to investigate Camilla's murder. But lucky for me, my self-preservation instinct kicked in before the words managed to tumble from my mouth.

"Have you seen either of Camilla's boys?" I asked, between bites of mashed potatoes and gravy. "I wanted to speak to them before I left."

"Only from a distance. They've been surrounded by so many people, I haven't been able to get close enough to offer my condolences." He abandoned stuffing his face for a moment, shifted closer to me, and sniffed the air. "What's that smell?"

I studied my plate. "Onions, garlic . . . possibly a touch of cinnamon."

He moved in closer, sniffed again.

Suddenly uncomfortable, I eased back, and bumped into the

dining room wall. Hoping to put more distance between us, I angled my plate out in front of me.

"Not onions. And definitely not garlic." He sniffed the air again. "More like . . . gardenias."

"Oh. My perfume. It's—"

"The same fragrance I gave you for Christmas our senior year of high school."

Searing heat began to inch up my neck. I felt like banging my head against the wall. What kind of idiot still wears the same perfume her high-school sweetheart gave her? Then lets him get close enough to recognize it?

"Remember how we used to sit on your front porch near that gardenia plant? How you said you wanted your bridal bouquet to be made from gardenias? That it was your favorite flower in the whole world."

I remembered all right. "That was a lifetime ago."

"Not really."

There was a sparkle in his eyes that I didn't trust. He eased closer, blocking my path of escape.

Pulse rate accelerating, I shot into crisis mode. Peering over his shoulder for a distraction, I zeroed in on Camilla's oldest son. "Hey, there's Tony. Didn't you say you needed to speak to him?"

He grinned. "Nice try."

"No, really." I nodded toward the hallway. "You're going to miss him if you don't hurry."

He looked around, spotted Tony moving through the crowd, and sighed. Like me, he was here for more than the food. "I'm afraid we'll have to continue this conversation later." He dumped his plate into the nearest trash can and hurried to catch up with Tony.

Acting on instinct, I tossed my plate into the trash and followed.

"Get lost," he said when I caught up with him.

"Dream on." I scooted past him, beating him to the room Tony had entered by a few seconds.

We found our quarry seated behind a large, mahogany desk near the window. He looked up in surprise as we bounded through the doorway. "I hope we're not interrupting," I said, only slightly out of breath.

If he was upset at the interruption, he did a good job of hiding it. "Not at all." A ray of sunlight cut through the spotless glass behind him, setting his close-cropped, copper hair gleaming. His brow puckered as he scanned his memory for a name. "Kate, isn't it?" he said, after a moment.

"That's right," I answered, surprised that he'd remembered. Nodding toward the grumpy looking man beside me, I added, "And this is Steven Griggs."

"Yes, of course." Tony's manners kicked in. He stood up and shook hands with Steven. "Thank you both for coming. Mother would have been pleased to see you both here."

There was a squareness about the man that was hard to miss. Broad, square shoulders; thick, square hands; and a solid, square chin. Only the bulbous nose dared defy the pattern.

Suddenly, his light-blue eyes flicked back and forth between us. "Are you two together again?"

That was the bad part about growing up in a small town, everyone knew your history. "Nope." I tried not to sound as irritated as I felt. "We just bumped into each other by the refreshment table."

"I see." There was a note of disbelief in his voice.

"No, really. We're not together. In fact, Steven here"—I jerked a thumb in his direction—"is engaged to Sissy Holmes."

"*Was* engaged to Sissy Holmes," Steven corrected.

"The Sissy Holmes whose dad owns half the town?" Tony wanted to know.

Steven nodded. "That would be the one."

I'd heard enough about Sissy Holmes. "My mother and aunt also wanted me to express their condolences to your family."

At the mention of the word "aunt," a light suddenly dawned in Tony's eyes. "Lula Mae Elkins. She's your aunt. How could I have forgotten that? I've heard Mother mention her name often enough."

Not in flattering terms, I'd bet. "They are . . . we are," I corrected, "so sorry about what happened to your mother."

Tony flicked a look toward Steven. "Didn't you arrest her aunt for stealing a pair of Mother's earrings?"

"We took Mrs. Elkins in for questioning," Steven agreed.

I struggled to keep my voice civil. "There's no evidence my aunt stole those earrings, or that they actually belonged to your mother."

Steven cleared his throat. "He confirmed they were hers this morning."

"I'm sure Camilla wasn't the only woman in town who owned a pair of earrings like that," I said, defending my position. "I'm sure every jewelry store in town sells them."

"My dad had those earrings custom made for Mother by a jeweler in New York," Tony replied.

"Well"—my frustration was beginning to show—"it was just an honest mistake on my aunt's part. When she found them outside her front door, she thought they were a gift from her fiancé."

Tony stared at me as if I'd recently escaped from some loony bin.

"Oh, for goodness sakes," I said. "They were wrapped in wedding paper. What was she supposed to think?"

"One of my guys did find wrapping paper wadded up in a trash can outside Lula Mae's house," Steven confirmed.

"There was something else . . ." Tony groped for the memory.

"Your aunt, I heard she was working with some guy, maybe this fiancé of hers, to steal Mother's money. My guess is, something went wrong and they killed her so she wouldn't go to the cops."

A surge of adrenaline shot through me. "That's the most ridiculous thing I've ever heard." Shifting into battle mode, I started around the desk. "Lula Mae would never—"

Steven grabbed my elbow and held on. "I don't think now is the time, or the place, to be discussing this matter."

Tony glared at him. "What kind of policeman are you, letting the woman who killed my mother run around free?"

"Mr. Davenport," Steven attempted to defuse the situation, "I realize you're upset, but I assure you, we're doing everything possible to find out who killed your mother."

"You already know who killed her."

In deference to the lawman standing next to me, I tried reasoning with the man. "Lula Mae is one of the kindest, most gentle human beings on earth." There was a dangerous edge to my voice that he would've had to be deaf to miss. "And I resent you talking about her like she's some low-life criminal. There's no way she'd ever harm anyone. Just because she happens to be engaged to that louse Percy Moss doesn't mean she—"

"Wait a minute. Back up," Tony said. "Run that by me again."

"What?" I was confused. "The part about her being the kindest, most—"

"No. No." He strode around the desk. "The part about her being engaged to this Moss fellow."

Maybe I'd missed something. "She is . . . was . . . engaged to Percy Moss."

"That's impossible." He shook his head. "We must be talking about two different people here. My mother called me a few days before"—the words seemed to get caught in his throat—"she passed. She told me she was getting married again. To a man named Percy Moss."

I can't say his revelation surprised me. I was on the verge of informing him about Percy's fondness for wealthy widows when a warning hand settled on my shoulder.

The transformation from average man to cop happened instantly. "Do you know if your mother was involved in any business dealings with Mr. Moss?" Steven asked, his sharp, gray eyes on alert.

"Uh . . ." Tony seemed to be caught off guard. "I'm not sure. Maybe."

"Did she ever say anything to you about investing in a bakery?"

"Not that I can remember."

"What about your brother?"

"What about him?"

The muscles in Steven's jaw tightened. "Do you think she mentioned anything to him about investing in a bakery?"

"I doubt it." Tony shook his head. "My brother's not exactly a genius when it comes to investment advice."

"And you are?" I couldn't resist the jab.

He glared at me. "As a matter of fact," he began, but broke off when a tall, elegant woman strode into the room.

The woman's long mass of platinum blond hair fell to her shoulders in a perfect wave. The slinky, black dress she had on screamed "designer label," and the band of emeralds around her neck looked real. Coming up beside Tony, she cast an inquisitive glance in our direction.

Tony introduced us. "Evelyn, this is Kate Spencer and Steven Griggs, old high-school classmates."

She smiled. "I'm amazed by how many of Tony's friends from high school showed up for the services."

I shrugged. "It's a small town."

"So I've noticed," Evelyn replied.

"Your husband was getting ready to tell us about his mother's business dealings with Percy Moss," Steven said.

Evelyn looked surprised. "Business dealings?" She glanced at Tony. "I thought your mother was engaged to the man."

"She was. At least," he amended, "that's what she told me on the phone the other night."

"Sheriff," Evelyn said, "you must realize by now that my mother-in-law had a great deal of money. I suggest you begin your investigation by delving into this fellow's background. Perhaps he—"

"It's Lieutenant," Steven corrected her, "and we're already looking into Mr. Moss's background." He paused a moment, and studied her closely. "What makes you think Percy Moss had anything to do with your mother-in-law's death?"

"Because it's the plot of a thousand movies," she said. "A stranger rolls into town, tries to con a wealthy widow out of her life savings by promising to marry her. When she realizes he has no intention of keeping his promise, she backs out of financing his business. In a fit of rage, he kills her, then sneaks out of town with all her cash, and whatever he can pawn. Then the cycle starts all over again in a new town."

"It's also possible," Steven said, "she loved the man and had no problem forking over the money to start up his bakery."

Though no one had asked for it, I decided to throw in an opinion of my own. "Seems to me, Percy would have been better off actually marrying Camilla than getting her to invest in his business. That way, when she . . . passed on . . . he could inherit all her money."

Tony's eyes morphed into ice-blue daggers. "Mother was not a foolish woman. She would never have left any of Father's money to some man she's known only a few months. Besides, she promised me—" He broke off abruptly.

"Promised you what?" Steven asked.

A shadow of sadness passed over Tony's face. "It doesn't

matter now."

Before Steven could pursue the matter, Evelyn tugged on Tony's arm. "Honey, I think it's time we got back to our other guests. I'm sure many of them are ready to pay their respects and be on their way."

"You're right, of course." The words tumbled from his mouth, as if they hovered near the surface, ready to pop out at a moment's notice.

"If you will excuse us," Evelyn said, and steered her husband toward the door.

Not ready to be dismissed, we trailed behind them, watching as they took their places near the front door. While Tony appeared uncomfortable, Evelyn performed her duties to perfection—making small talk, thanking each person for coming. Yet, I got the impression it was all an act. Maybe it had something to do with her eyes. They remained as hard and cold as the emeralds hanging around her neck.

While we stood there regarding the pair, Steven got a call on his cell phone and took off. Before I made my own departure, I decided to mosey back to the buffet table and snag another slice of peach pie. I was enjoying my little piece of heaven when I caught sight of Keith Davenport, Camilla's younger son, slipping out the French doors in the dining room.

Why wasn't he by the front door with the rest of the family? With a sigh of regret, I ditched the pie and trailed after him.

CHAPTER TWENTY

By the time I made it outside, Keith was huddled under a live oak tree near the back of the property, smoking a cigarette. Taller than his brother by several inches, he had his father's dark hair and coloring.

Leaving behind the comfort of pavement, I trudged across the lawn, my two-inch heels poking holes in the soft earth. Keith turned to watch my approach. "Mind if I join you?" I asked.

A smile oozed slowly and easily, like a drip of molasses, across his face. "I never say no to a beautiful lady."

Same old Keith, always trying to charm the ladies. "Remember me? Kate Spencer? We went to high school together?"

"Oh, right," he said, after giving it some thought. "You were in my algebra class. It's been a long time. I haven't thought about Mrs. Peabody in years. I wonder if she's still teaching."

"I heard she retired a couple of years ago."

"Thank goodness," he said. "I really hated that woman."

"Didn't we all."

We spent a few minutes reminiscing about some of the people we'd gone to high school with and what they were doing now, then I said, "I met Evelyn inside just now, but I guess I must have missed your wife. Someone told me she's from New York."

"Let's just say that's where she likes to spend my money." His voice had a harsh edge to it. "But you couldn't have missed her because she isn't here."

118

"I just assumed . . ."

"You, and everyone else in town." He made an effort to calm down. "Sorry. I didn't mean to bite your head off. The thing is, my wife and I, we're in the process of getting a divorce. Sometimes, I just go a little nuts talking about it."

"No harm done."

"I guess it's no big deal, really," he went on. "Marriages break up all the time, right? Probably half the population's in the same boat." His hand trembled slightly as he lit up another cigarette. "How about you? Married? Have any kids?"

"No to both questions."

"Consider yourself lucky then. My kids are in New York with their mother, who didn't feel they ought to be subjected to anything so distasteful as death." His brow knotted together. "Even though it's their own grandmother we're talking about here."

"How old are they?"

"Tyler's six, and Kyle's ten."

"I imagine things have been pretty tough for them."

"I suppose. But hey," he said, trying to sound optimistic, "they say kids are very resilient. I guess we're about to find out."

"By the time you're through, I suppose this divorce could wind up costing you big bucks."

"Tell me about it. I'm looking at alimony and child-support payments. Hopefully, I'll get lucky and some rich dude will come along and take Barbara off my hands."

"But you'll still be stuck with child-support payments."

He cocked up a bushy brow. "Whose side are you on?"

"I'm not on anyone's side." I knew the smart thing to do would be to back down, but something inside made me press on. "I suppose with your mother gone, money isn't going to be a problem anymore."

"My luck, Barbara will wind up with half of that, too."

Remembering the expensive-looking specimen by Tony's side, I played a hunch. "I'm sure Tony's inheritance couldn't have come at a better time."

Keith reached out and grabbed my arm. "Why would you think he needs money?"

I tried to ignore the flash of pain that shot up my arm. "No reason really."

He seemed to realize he was hurting me and let go of my arm. "Look, I know there have been some ugly rumors going around about Davenport Hardware being in trouble. But hey, that's all they are—rumors. Believe me, his business is rock solid."

There was an underlying tension behind his words that made me wonder what he was hiding. "But if his business was in trouble," I said, "your mother's death probably takes care of most of his cash-flow problems."

Keith's eyes narrowed. "What are you implying?"

"Nothing." I slapped on my best innocent look. "It's just that your mother's death is going to leave both you and your brother pretty well off."

"So?"

I shrugged. "So, nothing. Just thinking out loud."

Taking a step forward, he got right in my face. "If my family's name gets dragged through the mud by a bunch of gossipy women, I'll know who to blame."

An eternity seemed to pass. Finally, he stepped back, gave a curt nod, then strode toward the house.

I didn't feel all that proud of myself for goading him into a response as I ambled around to the front yard to reclaim my truck. But I consoled myself with the thought that I was helping Lula Mae. And she was family.

CHAPTER TWENTY-ONE

The next morning, the radio was blaring in the background as I separated another clump of aloe and potted up the pieces. While my hands were busy working, my mouth was busy pretending to be a rock star. On the parts where I actually knew the words, I joined in, singing with enthusiasm, if not much talent.

But I didn't care. There was no one around to hear me. Or so I thought.

A loud knock on the screen door, which separated the working side of the greenhouse from the customer portion, told me otherwise. I immediately quit singing and swung around to see who was there.

To my surprise, Evelyn Davenport stood in the doorway. Today she was tucked into a pair of tight black slacks and a confetti-sprinkled silk blouse. "I can come back if you're busy," she said.

"No, that's okay." I slipped off the pink, cotton gloves I wore to protect my hands and flipped off the radio. "I was getting ready to take a break anyway." Slipping through the door to join her, I added cautiously, "What can I do for you?"

The cool, collected woman I'd met yesterday must have been an illusion. The one today flitted up and down the aisles like some caged bird searching for a way out. "Are these hard to grow?" She stopped long enough to poke a finger at a Chlorophytum sonosum, or spider plant, as most people know them.

"Actually they're one of the best plants for beginners," I told her, and launched into my usual spiel on its care, even though I was fairly certain she wasn't listening.

"How about this one?" She moved over and picked up a Saintpaulia inonatha, or African violet.

Once again, I gave her a little background information, then went over its care. We continued the charade several more times before she got around to the real reason she was here. "By the way, Keith mentioned that you'd heard some ugly rumors about Davenport Hardware."

"Maybe a few." My reply was deliberately vague, hopefully giving her the impression I knew more than I did. Which, if I was forced to tell the truth, the whole truth, and nothing but the truth, would be, I hadn't heard squat.

"You do realize that's all they are—rumors?"

I shrugged. "That's what Keith said."

I could see the struggle going on inside her. "Okay." She lowered her voice, taking me into her confidence. "So maybe the business is going through a few problems at the moment. But it's nothing we can't handle." Her restless hands sought comfort in the leaves of a Dieffenbachia, making me itch to snatch it out of her grasp and send her packing.

"I admit," she went on, "the money Tony stands to inherit from his mother's estate will be a blessing. But if it wasn't there, we'd get a loan from the bank, or a line of credit with our suppliers to tide us over until business picks up again. Which it will." The last was spoken with such force that I had no doubt, if it were humanly possible, Davenport Hardware would rise from the grave on her say-so alone.

"Look." I decided to be straight with her. "I'm not accusing you or Tony of anything. I'm simply trying to make sure my aunt doesn't get blamed for something she didn't do."

"That's funny, because it sounds to me like that's exactly what you're doing—accusing one of us of murdering Camilla.

And I don't like it. Not one bit. And I suggest that, from now on, you stay out of our business." There was a dangerous edge to her voice that made my blood run cold.

But I didn't back down. "All I'm trying to do is clear my aunt's name."

"Look, I'm not naïve." She changed tactics. "I know that even in the best of families sometimes one member commits an atrocious act against another. But I can assure you that it isn't the case this time. I know Tony. He loved his mother. He would never kill her. Especially not for money."

"Put yourself in my place," I said. "I know Lula Mae didn't kill anybody. So that means somebody else did. Somebody the police must be overlooking."

"You mean somebody who stands to gain by Camilla's death?" Her words were laced with sarcasm.

I rolled my eyes. "It's not rocket science."

Her chin jutted out. A dangerous glint appeared in those green eyes. An instinct for self-preservation had me backing away. I grabbed the trowel I'd been using to pot aloe, ready to defend myself if she came at me.

"Tony did not kill his mother," she said slowly, flexing her shoulders as if readying for combat. "And anyone who goes around implying otherwise will have to answer to me."

We stood there an endless moment, neither of us willing to back down.

"Look," she said, her voice softening, "maybe we can come to some sort of agreement."

I eyed her suspiciously. "What sort of an agreement?"

"You must realize we can't afford the slightest blemish on our reputation right now. Our customers and suppliers need to have absolute confidence in our integrity and ability to meet our obligations."

I thought I knew where she was headed. "You're not suggesting what I think you are?"

She lifted a brow. "How much will it take?"

I stood there, shocked by what I was hearing.

A complacent smile settled on her face as she waited for my answer.

I took great pleasure in knocking it off. "No way, lady. I'd never let my aunt go to jail for something she didn't do. Not for all the money in the world. And furthermore, I'm beginning to wonder if there isn't more to this Tony-killing-his-mother-business than I thought."

Her face hardened. "Let me give you a piece of friendly advice. Don't cross me, or you might live to regret it." She waited a moment for her words to sink in, then whirled around and stomped toward the door.

I raced after her, steam practically shooting from my ears. I caught up with her near the outer door. "Just who do you think you're dealing with—a moron? The police are bound to check out the financial condition of Davenport Hardware, if they haven't done so already. And when they do, you'll be in a heap of trouble."

She didn't defend her position, just tossed me a wicked grin, then yanked open the door and sailed through, letting it slam in my face.

The nerve of that woman!

As she sashayed toward her car, I jerked open the door and yelled, "Don't think you're going to get rid of me that easily. I'll keep digging until I know everything there is to know about you Davenports."

Once she disappeared from sight, I made an effort to calm down, slowly counting from one to a hundred. At least that was the plan. I made it to sixty-five, then jammed on my gloves and went back to potting aloe.

But I was too keyed up to settle down to such a mundane

task. Ripping off the gloves, I took off walking, hoping to burn off some of the unbridled energy pulsing through my body.

CHAPTER TWENTY-TWO

We were clustered around the TV watching a rerun of one of our favorite crime shows when Happy leaned back and let out an enormous yawn. Getting to her feet, she stretched her arms overhead, popping and crackling worse than a bowl of puffed rice cereal. "I'm bushed," she said. "I think I'll turn in early."

"Aren't you going to finish watching our program?" Lula Mae asked. "We're almost to the part where—"

"I said I was bushed," Happy snapped.

Lula Mae's eyes flew open. "Oh, me, too." She leaped to her feet and went through the same routine of yawning and stretching that Happy had. "Why, I'm so sleepy I can barely keep my eyes open."

What was going on here? I glanced at the clock. It was barely seven-thirty. "You two can't be sleepy already."

"It's been a long day," Happy said. "Come on, Lula Mae, you've been looking kind of puffy lately. I've got some eye cream you can use."

Once they were gone, I sat there a few minutes staring at the TV set, then reached over and snapped it off. I'd already seen this episode myself. Besides, it was no fun watching alone.

It wasn't until I was on my way upstairs that it hit me—with the two of them tucked in bed, I could scoot over to Percy's and do a little snooping, maybe find the stash of Uncle George's things he'd *borrowed* from Lula Mae. If luck was with me, Mrs. Peterson would be so engrossed in her TV programs, she wouldn't go calling the cops again to report an intruder.

To keep the crime sisters off my trail, I went through the whole charade of preparing for bed: brushing my teeth, removing my makeup, changing into my pajamas. But as soon as the bedroom door closed, off came the pajamas and on went the jeans and T-shirt. Since I could still hear Happy and Lula Mae shuffling about, I grabbed a book off the dresser and settled on the bed to wait.

Half an hour later, the house quieted down. Being cautious, I cracked open the bedroom door and listened for sounds of anyone still moving about. Except for the steady hum of the air conditioner and the occasional creak of the house settling, all was quiet.

I was tugging on my sneakers when I heard a noise in the hallway. I barely had time to scramble over and ease the door closed before footsteps shuffled past.

"Are you sure we ought to be doing this?" Lula Mae whispered, loud enough to wake King Tut.

"You said you wanted to find out if . . ." Happy's words died out as they moved on.

Why those two old coots! Just where did they think they were going? I gave them ten seconds, then pounded down the stairs after them.

Slipping out the front door, I ducked behind an azalea bush and watched as the two climbed into the Blue Bomber. When the overhead light flashed on, I could see that they were dressed for the occasion in dark sweats. The motor soon hummed to life and they chugged down the driveway, flattening an entire row of monkey grass in the process. When they reached the road, Happy made a sharp left, barely missing the light post.

Praying I hadn't just let Godzilla loose on the town, I scrambled into my truck and took off after them, not turning on my lights until another car cut between us.

After a few minutes, I realized where they were headed and eased up on the gas. Two blocks from Percy's house, Happy slammed on the brakes and pulled over, bumping into the curb. I managed a last-minute turn down Sycamore, narrowly avoiding detection.

By the time I found a parking spot and hiked back to River Road, the two of them had taken possession of Percy's front porch. Lula Mae was down on her knees, running a hand along the underside of the porch. With only the puny light of a distant street lamp to see by, it took her a few minutes to locate the object she was after. "My arthritis is killing me," she complained as she grabbed the railing to hoist herself up.

"Hurry up." Happy opened the screen door. "We ain't got all night. You want Mrs. Peterson to see us skulking around out here again and call the police?"

"Here." Lula Mae thrust the key at her. "If you're in such an almighty hurry, you open the door."

"All right, I will." Happy snatched the key from Lula Mae's hand and began to fumble around, trying to locate the keyhole.

What a perfect opportunity to teach the two of them a lesson they wouldn't soon forget.

Using the overgrown shrubbery for cover, I crept forward. When I came within a few feet of them, I called out, "Think you two are making enough noise?"

In the stillness, my voice sounded like the boom of a shotgun blast. The two of them began to squeal like a couple of frightened pigs. Happy dropped the key, and Lula Mae charged toward me waving her flashlight. "Stay back," she warned. "Don't come any closer, or I'll bash your brains in."

I believed her all right. Enough to back up a few steps. "Hey, it's only me, your sweet, loving niece."

Lula Mae's arm sagged to her side in relief. Happy flew across the porch and swatted my shoulder. "What's the matter with you? Are you trying to give me a heart attack?"

I folded my hands across my chest and glared at her. "The next time you two decide to play detective, how about not sneaking off without me. Because"—I included Lula Mae in my glare—"neither one of you is any good at keeping a low profile."

Folding her hands across her own chest, Happy glared back. "Are you trying to test my patience?"

Lula Mae had the good sense to intervene. "Are we aiming to stand here jawing all night, or are we going inside and taking a look around?"

Happy was the first to thaw. "I guess there's no sense in us standing here all night."

Hiding a smile, I bent down, retrieved the key, and slipped it into the keyhole on my first try. On the way inside, I snagged Percy's mail from the rickety box beside the door.

Hot air immediately bombarded us. Evidently, Percy was frugal enough to switch off the air conditioner before hightailing it out of town. Already, beads of sweat were forming on my upper lip.

"For lands sakes, Lula Mae," Happy said, "turn the air conditioner on. I feel like a stuffed pig in here."

And sounded like one a few minutes ago, I thought with a smile.

"What are you smiling about?" Happy demanded.

I ditched the smile and pulled out my own flashlight. "Nothing."

"Well then, don't just stand there twiddling your thumbs—get busy. We ain't got all night." She jabbed a finger into my chest. "After you sort through that pile of mail, check out the bedroom. Lula Mae, you tackle the kitchen. I'll take the living room."

Without complaint, I trotted off to do her bidding.

There was nothing interesting in the mail, mostly just a bunch of sales papers. I tossed it on the bed, then got busy searching the dresser. Where I made a startling discovery: Percy was the most compulsive neat freak I'd ever come across. His socks were neatly arranged in his drawer by color. His underwear was stacked in orderly piles. Handkerchiefs and pajamas each had their own drawer. Everything was so organized, I began to wonder if Percy had kept a get-away bag stashed someplace.

Next, I tackled the closet, where I found a dozen starched and pressed shirts hanging on the left side, matching pants on the right. The only deviation from this overly neat obsession appeared to be his closet shelf. It was buried under a mound of hats. From what I could see, most of them baseball caps. But there was this one—a black cowboy hat. Curious to see how I'd look as a cowgirl, I reached up and snatched it off the shelf. As I did, a small, red notebook tumbled to the floor.

I tossed the hat back on the shelf and reached for the notebook. Quickly thumbed through the pages. Neatly printed names began to pop out at me. Names I knew. Like Fran Parker and Camilla Davenport. And underneath each name were carefully written notations about their backgrounds, approximate net worth, and how much money he'd conned, or planned to con, each woman out of. I had just reached Lula Mae's entry when I heard movement in the hallway. Making a snap decision, I jammed the notebook into the front of my jeans and hid its bulk with my T-shirt.

From the sound of all the grumbling going on, I took it neither of them had found anything of importance. Not Uncle George's things. And certainly nothing that would tell us where Percy might be hiding out. "The man might as well have been living in some motel," Happy said, "for all the personality this place has."

An incredulous look crossed Lula Mae's face. "Can you believe it? He has the canned goods arranged in alphabetical order." She shook her head in disbelief.

"Imagine what your life would have been like married to such a neat freak," Happy said as we went out the door. She immediately launched into a tirade about some man she'd seen years ago on a talk show.

I walked with them back to Happy's car. "I'll be home as soon as I fill up my truck," I said. Neither one of them appeared to be listening. To test my theory, I added, "I'll try not to run into a deer on my way home and mangle my truck. Maybe hit the dashboard, give myself a concussion, and wind up in the emergency room."

Ignoring me, they hopped off on another tangent. This time about some kid they saw on another talk show who was a compulsive hand washer. Making my escape from the talk show queens, I trotted down Sycamore.

Across the street from where I'd parked my truck, a toy poodle was taking care of business on the front lawn. An old man stood on the porch waiting. Both man and dog spotted me about the same time. The dog started yelping and lunged across the street ready to defend his territory. The old man hobbled down the steps and yelled for the dog to stay. Not waiting around to find how well trained the animal was, I broke into a run, beating the little mutt to my truck just in the nip of time.

Before driving away, I pulled the notebook out of my waistband and jammed it into the glove compartment. Once I had time to study it, I'd find some way to get it to the police without incriminating myself.

Strike that last thought. Lula Mae's name was in that book. I couldn't possibly turn it over to the police and give them any more ammunition against her. Not if I wanted to continue breathing another day.

CHAPTER TWENTY-THREE

On the way home, I stopped at the nearest convenience store to feed my gas tank. As I stood there, nozzle in hand, I happened to glance across the street and spotted Jolene's red MG turning into the parking lot of Chuck's Steakhouse. Here was my chance to find out more about her dream man. Keeping my gaze glued to the passenger side of her car like an eager child on Christmas morning, I nearly fell over when I saw Keith Davenport, the grieving son of Camilla Davenport, emerge.

Only he didn't look all that grieving at the moment. Sweeping around the car, he hauled off and kissed Jolene right there in the middle of the parking lot. And I'm not talking about some little peck on the cheek either.

I was so surprised, I pulled the nozzle out and gas spewed everywhere. Even my normally quick reflexes couldn't save my sneakers. Not only did they take a good soaking, but so did the bottom of my jeans.

By the time I'd cleaned up, with the help of a few dozen paper towels, then bought a soda and a bag of chips from the harried clerk, the loving twosome had disappeared. Making one of those snap decisions that usually land me in trouble, I scooted across the intersection, pulled into the empty parking space next to Jolene's MG, and marched inside.

In all the excitement, I'd forgotten about the delightful fragrance of gasoline, which clung to my clothes. The hostess took one sniff, then wrinkled her nose in disgust. "Will anyone be joining you this evening?" she asked, holding her breath and trying to speak at the same time.

Before I could answer, someone stepped up behind me and said, "We'll take a booth. Preferably, one by the window."

I spun around to find Steven grinning at me. The hostess waited a beat to see if I offered any objections. When I didn't, she led us to one of the booths along the front wall.

Before plopping down, I scanned the area for Jolene and Keith. No sign of them. They must have opted for the back section.

The lady in the booth across from us shot an admiring glance Steven's way, but he didn't seem to notice. That prompted me to take a closer look at how he was dressed: neatly pressed, white shirt; blue dress pants; red silk tie.

My grubby jeans and over-sized T-shirt were certainly no match for his fashionable look. Not to mention the aroma of gasoline, which surrounded me. For a moment, I seriously considered crawling under the table.

He must have sensed how I felt, because he leaned forward and laid his hand over mine. "You look fine. As for your perfume . . ."

I felt my face grow hot and jerked my hand away. "Look, I wasn't really planning to—" I began, but broke off when a slender woman with cascades of rich auburn hair approached our booth.

"Sorry I'm late." She shifted her briefcase to her left hand, then placed her right hand on the top of his shoulder.

"No problem." He stood up so she could scoot in beside him. "I just arrived myself."

What an idiot I was! Of course, the man was meeting someone. Hoping to slip away quietly, I eased to the edge of the seat and, somehow, managed to knock over my water glass in the process. So much for a smooth getaway.

Before too much damage could be done, Steven righted my glass, then began to blot up the spill with his napkin. Fiery heat consumed my face, as an apology spilled from my mouth. I shot to my feet, ready to flee.

Steven laid a hand on my arm. "Going somewhere?"

"I just remembered that I was supposed to meet a friend of mine at Bessie's. Maybe if I hurry I can still catch him."

He called my bluff. "Why don't you go call this friend of yours and have him meet you here instead?"

If there had been a friend waiting for me, the ice in the redhead's eyes told me what my answer had better be. "Maybe some other time." Before he could object, I jerked my arm free, then scurried out of the restaurant like a spooked mouse being chased by a hungry cat.

Feeling thoroughly humiliated, I crawled inside my truck and rested my forehead against the cool surface of the steering wheel.

There came a tap at the window.

My head jerked up so fast, I probably could add a bad case of whiplash to my complaints.

Steven stood beside my truck looking pleased with himself. He motioned for me to roll down the window. Muttering a few choice words, I obliged.

He planted his paws on either side of the opening and stuck his head inside. The clean, citrus smell of his aftershave stung the air. "Come back inside and join us for dinner."

"No, really, I've got to—"

"Meet your friend." His bushy brows inched up. "Cut out the games. I've known you too long. We both know there's no friend waiting for you at Bessie's. Come back inside and have something to eat."

"Okay, so maybe I'm only rushing home to see Happy and Lula Mae, but I already told them I was on my way home. Trust me, if I don't arrive in the next ten minutes, they'll probably send out a posse to search for me."

He reached into his coat pocket and pulled out his cell phone. "Call and tell them to cancel the posse. You're with me."

I eyed the phone with disgust. "You know how I feel about those things. Besides, the only reason I came inside in the first place was because I saw Jolene and Keith Davenport go inside."

He looked puzzled. "As far as I know there's no law against two people having dinner."

How dense could the man be?

"Tell me, how does Keith know her? Before his mother's funeral, he hadn't been back to Port Springs in years."

He shrugged. "He probably ran into her around town somewhere. They got to talking, like people do in small towns. He asked her out. Simple as that." His face puckered in thought. "As I recall, she's not a bad-looking woman, just a bit scatterbrained for my taste."

I rapped on the steering wheel with the palm of my hand. Too bad I couldn't do the same to the man's head.

"Okay." He gave in. "Maybe you have a point. I'll check into the matter first thing in the morning. Better yet, come back inside with me and we'll—"

"No way," I said. "If Jolene sees me, she'll think I'm trying to butt into her business again."

His brows shot up. "And that just occurred to you?"

I ignored his comment and cranked up the engine. "Anyway, I don't think the redhead would be too pleased."

A devilish glint lit his eyes. "Jealous?"

I tilted my chin up. "Certainly not."

"Good," he said as I backed out, "because my relationship with her is strictly business."

Right. And my mother is on a mission to bring about world peace.

CHAPTER TWENTY-FOUR

By the time I made it home, I was in a foul mood. Thankfully, Happy and Lula Mae had already gone to bed. For real this time. I kicked off my shoes and stomped to the kitchen to fix myself a grilled cheese sandwich.

How could I have been so stupid? I flung a chunk of butter into an iron skillet. I must have looked like a total idiot at the restaurant. I tucked a piece of cheese between two slices of bread, then dumped it into the skillet.

Why did I care who Steven J. Griggs—make that Lieutenant Griggs—had dinner with? He didn't mean anything me to. As far as I was concerned, he was history.

Ancient history.

Ancient, ancient history.

When the cheese melted, I tossed the sandwich onto a plate and added a couple of dill pickles. Granted, the woman sharing his meal was fairly attractive. I slammed the plate onto the table. Okay, so maybe she was drop-dead gorgeous. She also knew how to dress well and had all the poise of a super model. So what?

A knock at the kitchen door saved me from any more ruminating. Padding across the room in my bare feet, I jerked open the door only to find Mr. Ancient History planted not two feet from my face. "What do you want?" I asked, ready to slam the door in his face.

"To talk."

"What, the redhead doesn't talk?"

"She talks," he answered calmly, "but we're finished with our business."

"Trying to set a world record for the shortest date in history?"

His chin jutted out. "I told you, it wasn't a date. We had—"

"Yeah, I know—business to discuss."

"Mind if I come in so we can talk about this like rational adults?"

He didn't look as if he'd accept no for an answer. "Suit yourself." I stepped away from the door.

"For your information," he launched into his explanation, "Cynthia is a real estate agent. *My* real estate agent. I'm buying the old Martin place."

"Since when do real estate agents go out on dates with their clients?"

"I told you, it wasn't a date."

"Looked like one to me."

He groaned. "Well, it wasn't. She just had some figures to go over with me."

"At this time of the night?" I couldn't keep the skepticism from my voice.

"In case you haven't noticed, I've been a little busy lately. And I wanted to get this thing wrapped up before someone else snatches up the place."

"And you couldn't meet her at her office because . . . ?" I waited for an explanation.

He shrugged. "I could have, but since she was planning on meeting her boyfriend at Chuck's, I thought I'd just meet her there, save her the trouble of opening the office back up."

I just bet she planned on meeting her boyfriend at Chuck's. The boyfriend she hoped to snag. Namely, Steven J. Griggs.

"What's wrong with your apartment?" I asked.

"What?" He seemed confused by my question.

"You heard me. What's wrong with your apartment?"

"Nothing is wrong with my apartment. At least, nothing that I know of."

That's when I pounced. "Then why the sudden interest in real estate?"

Understanding dawned. "Because I'm ready to settle down," he shot back. "Because I want a place of my own. Somewhere I can grow a few vegetables, putter around in the tool shed—that sort of stuff."

There was a definite ache in my chest. "So the wedding's back on?"

Irritation clouded his voice. "Can't a guy buy a house without everyone assuming he's headed to the altar?"

"Forget it." My desire for grill cheese morphed into a sudden urge for chocolate. "Hungry?"

"Starving." The wolfish gleam in his eyes made me nervous.

"Happy just made some of those double chocolate brownies you used to love so much," I said, steering him toward the table.

While I busied myself making coffee, he wandered over to the set of shelves that housed Happy's collection of antique food tins. "I don't remember this one." He pointed to a mustard tin.

"She got that one for her birthday last year." I set two mugs of coffee and a platter of brownies on the table.

Steven hightailed it back to the table. "Mmm," he sighed, as he bit into one of those thick, chewy pieces of heaven. "I'd forgotten how good these are. I don't suppose you ever learned to cook?"

"Not all of us are the domestic type."

"True. But a woman who can cook like this could have a dozen men standing in line, begging her to marry them."

"If she wanted to get married."

"If she wanted to get married," he conceded. "Which I'm sure you'd never consider."

"I never said that."

There was speculation in his eyes. "You never made it to the altar."

My appetite vanished. I dropped the brownie in my hand—my third, but who's counting—to my plate. "It's not that I don't want to get married. It's just that, I don't think I'd be any good at it." There, it was out. The damage done. "Like you said, a man wants a woman who can cook and sew and do all those things around the house that women do."

"Not every man is looking for a woman who wants to stay home and keep house." He took my hand in his. "Some of us actually like strong, independent women."

"You mean stubborn."

"That, too." He leaned forward. "Maybe we could try the dating thing. See how it goes."

I freed my hand. "You can't be serious."

"You don't have to sound so horrified."

I took a deep breath to steady myself. "When?"

He smiled. A big, wide smile that made his whole face glow. "Tomorrow night. Say, seven o'clock?"

I took a deep breath, then nodded.

Before I could change my mind, he snatched a couple of brownies off the platter and was out the door.

CHAPTER TWENTY-FIVE

The following morning, I called Jolene and asked her to come in, knowing that sometime during the day I'd figure out a way to pump her for information about her new boyfriend.

She finally sauntered in an hour later, her well-endowed body tucked into a tight pair of jeans and a blue flowered top. And, to be honest, she looked awful. Her large, brown eyes were bloodshot, and she shuffled about like some old lady.

"Had a rough night?" I asked, debating whether to send her packing for some much need R and R, or get on with my grilling.

She yawned. "I'm just a little tired, that's all."

"Maybe you should try sleeping at night."

"Hey," she said. "I've had a lot on my mind these last few weeks."

She was making this too easy. "Let me guess, the new boyfriend."

A smile lit her face. "You wouldn't believe how good looking he is. I'm talking on a scale of one to ten, he's definitely a twelve."

"If he's that great, how could I have missed bumping into him? Port Springs isn't that big a place."

She thought about it. "Maybe you don't hang out in the right places."

Was she implying that I was too old to hang out with all the really cool people?

That was absurd. I wasn't old. Old was—Happy and Lula Mae.

"His name's Keith Davenport and—" She went on to describe him, but I had a hard time paying attention. I was still stuck on her remark about not hanging out in the right places.

"Wait a minute." I forced my attention back to the task at hand. "Are we talking about Camilla Davenport's son?" I crossed my fingers, hoping no one had enlightened her about the whole Lula Mae/Camilla thing.

She shoved back a lock of blonde hair, which was beginning to show dark roots. "Isn't it just awful?" Her freckled little nose wrinkled. "I mean, the poor guy's mother gets murdered right in her own home. Can you believe it?"

"It's too bad you never got to meet her," I said, trying to sound sympathetic.

"Yeah, Keith wanted to introduce us a couple of times, but you know me, I don't get along too well with those society types."

"How's that possible?" I was sure my math wasn't that rusty. "I mean, Keith didn't get into town until a few days ago."

She looked at me funny.

"At least," I amended, "I assume he came in for his mother's funeral."

"Actually, Keith and I have been dating for almost a month now." She checked the date on her watch. "As a matter of fact, tomorrow will be our one-month anniversary."

There must be some mistake. "Keith couldn't possibly have been in town that long. Someone would've noticed him."

"Well, I noticed him. And everyone at Tio's noticed him. And since he's been living in one of those cabins out by the lake, whoever runs the place must've noticed him." Her face took on a dreamy look. "I must say, we've had some mighty fine times

141

on that lake. Did you know that they rent paddle boats out there?"

Wait a minute! Keith was living in one of those cabins out by the lake where Percy's car had been found. Could he have something to do with Percy's disappearance?

I'd have to give it some serious thought. In the meantime, I needed to convince my employee to keep her distance from the man.

"Jolene," I said, when she paused for air, "do you really think you should be hanging out with this guy? If I'm not mistaken, he's married."

"They're getting a divorce." Her words carried the ring of conviction.

I rolled my eyes. "Let me guess. His wife doesn't understand him. She—" I broke off, noticing her body stiffen.

"For your information"—she flounced over to a table of marigolds and began to pluck off dead blooms—"Keith has already started the paperwork. And you're right, his wife doesn't understand him. Here she is, married to a great guy, and she doesn't appreciate him."

"But you do?"

"You bet I do. He's my soul mate. The man I've been waiting all my life to find. And I'm not about to blow it by listening to a bunch of busybodies, who have no idea what they're talking about."

I moved around the table to face her. "What does his family think about your romance?"

She looked away. "We haven't told them."

"Doesn't that tell you something?" I asked gently.

"All it tells me is," she said, marching over and beginning to unravel the hose, "he needs time to prepare his family. They're dealing with a lot right now."

Realizing I was fighting a losing battle, I gave up and headed back to the office. Before I could get far, she called out, "I'll need to take a long lunch break today."

I spun back around. "Take all the time you need," I said, eager to make amends. Then spoiled whatever goodwill I'd earned by adding, "What's up? Another date with Mr. Dreamboat?"

She tossed me a look guaranteed to wilt every plant in the place, then snapped off the hose and stalked toward the greenhouse.

After that, I didn't have much time to worry about any hard feelings. The garden center was hit by a swarm of customers, all needing help "right now." The one time our paths did cross, I overheard her tell her friend, the one who was forever hanging around and was only tolerated because Jolene was such a good worker, about her lunch date at the Harbor Lights.

As it so happened, around eleven I got this sudden urge to try something different for lunch myself. Something that only an upscale place like the Harbor Lights would serve.

CHAPTER TWENTY-SIX

Fortunately, the Harbor Lights wasn't crowded so I had no trouble spotting Keith. He was nestled at a table near the window, sipping a glass of iced tea. His attention seemed to be focused on all the activity along the dock. Waving aside the hostess, who rushed over to seat me, I made a beeline for his table.

Sensing a presence, Keith looked around, an expectant smile lighting his face. Bright sunlight streaming through the wall of glass beside him made the lines fanning his green eyes more noticeable. "Uh, Kate." The smile died. "I'd ask you to join me, but I'm meeting someone. In fact"—his eyes swept past me and settled on the entrance as if he expected this person to magically appear—"she should be arriving any minute."

"If you're waiting on Jolene, I'm afraid she'll be awhile."

His gaze slid back to me. "But she—"

"Left a message with Jake for you to meet her early."

"How would you know that?" He sounded suspicious.

"Mind if I sit down?" Without waiting for approval, I slid into the seat across from him. "Because I'm the one who left it."

"I wondered why Jolene called the manager's office instead of my cell phone. I figured she forgot to recharge her phone again and couldn't remember the number." He studied me. "Care to tell me what this is about?"

I tried to decide where to begin. "As you probably know, Jolene works for me down at the garden center."

He shook his head. "She told me she was a student at the junior college."

"Well, she is. But when she's not in class, she works for me. Look," I said, trying to think of a delicate way to say what was on my mind, "I don't usually get involved in my employees' personal lives, but I'm making an exception this time. I don't think this relationship you two have is good for Jolene."

"How is our relationship any of your business?"

"You probably don't know this, but Jolene's had quite a few relationships that didn't work out."

"Just because Jolene's had trouble in the past, doesn't mean our relationship is doomed."

"Correct me if I'm wrong, but the last time I checked you weren't in any position to put a ring on her finger."

He frowned. "I'm taking care of that problem."

"Sure you are. Until you realize how much money the divorce is going to cost you, and you decide to reconcile with your wife."

"You listen to me." He struggled to contain his anger. "Jolene and I have a good thing going. And I don't intend to let you, or anybody else, mess this up."

"What about your wife? I bet you two had a good thing going once, too. And look how that turned out."

He squirmed in his seat. "My marriage was over long before I met Jolene. Cindy and I, we want different things out of life. She likes to hang out with those artsy, creative types. Me, I like to hang out with more down-to-earth people. That's why Jolene's so perfect for me; she's so . . . grounded."

I changed tactics, taking him by surprise. "I bet your mother wasn't all that pleased to hear about the divorce."

He cocked his head to one side and began to massage the muscles around the base of his neck. "It's understandable, I guess," he finally said. "Cindy was the daughter she never had.

To be honest, when Mother found out about the divorce, she called Cindy and gave her this big speech about how destructive a divorce would be for the kids. She felt if we just hung in there, got some marriage counseling, everything would work out." He snorted, clearly showing his assessment of that idea.

"I take it you didn't agree."

He shook his head. "Cindy's a great gal. She's the mother of my children, for goodness sakes. But she isn't the right woman for me. These past twelve years have been a living nightmare. I think the real reason Mother wanted us to stay together is that she could control Cindy; therefore, she could control me."

Having a rather strong-willed mother myself, my sympathy went out to him. But I didn't let it stop me. "I suppose your mother's not going to be a problem anymore."

"What is it with you?" His lips thinned into almost nothingness. "Get this straight. I did not kill my mother. I have no idea who did. Maybe it was that Moss character. Maybe it was your aunt. But it wasn't me."

"Then why have you been hiding out at the lake all this time?"

I'd caught him by surprise again. "How did you . . . No." He held up a hand. "Let me guess. Jolene told you." He leaned back in his seat. "So I've been back in town for several weeks. There's no law against that. And instead of staying in town, I rented one of those cabins out by the lake. Not because I was plotting to kill my mother. Far from it. I came to protect her."

It was my turn to be surprised. "Protect her from what?"

He hesitated, as if debating with himself how much to say. "About a month ago, I got this call from her. She wanted to let me know she was getting married again. I have to tell you, the news came as quite a shock. I mean, I never thought about her getting married again. Not after the way she kept hanging on to Dad's memory. Reminding us over and over again how wonderful he was."

I recalled my own reaction to Lula Mae's wedding plans and found my resolve to pin the murder on Keith weakening.

"This guy she told me about sounded a little too good to be true," he went on. "So I put in for some vacation time and came down to check things out for myself. I wanted to make sure this guy wasn't trying to swindle her out of all the money Dad left her."

It made perfect sense to me. Family was . . . family. You protected those you loved.

"Considering his relationship with your aunt," he said, "it was a good thing I did."

"That doesn't explain the cabin. Wouldn't it have made more sense to stay with your mother, where you could get a firsthand look at the guy?"

"And have her figure out what I was up to?" He rolled his eyes. "I'm not stupid."

The waitress sauntered over with our menus. Keith brusquely informed her that we were waiting for someone to join us. "We'll order when she arrives."

As the waitress scurried back to the kitchen, I leaned forward and hit him with the big question. "Did you stop by the house the night your mother was killed?"

He suddenly became fascinated with the silverware. Finally, he said, "I dropped by earlier in the evening. I thought I might join her for dinner."

"And?" I waited for him to elaborate.

He returned the fork to its proper place and met my gaze. "There was a car in the driveway, so I parked down the street and slipped in through the kitchen. Imagine my surprise when I saw your aunt in the living room with Mother." His eyebrows arched up. "I didn't know they were speaking to each other."

"What about Percy?" I asked. "Was his car in driveway? Did you see him in the living room with your mother and Lula Mae?"

He shook his head. "There was nobody there but the two of them."

"Percy was planning to have dinner with your mother that night. Maybe he was hiding out in one of the bedrooms, waiting for Lula Mae to leave."

"Like I said, there was only one car in the driveway. An old yellow Cadillac. And the whole time I was there, I never heard the sound of a man's voice." He leaned back in his seat. "Of course, from the way my mother and your aunt were going at it, he probably couldn't have gotten a word in if he tried."

"You make it sound as if they were at each other's throats when, most likely, they were merely having a loud discussion."

"Believe me, this was no loud discussion. 'At each other's throats' is a more accurate description. From what I gathered, each one seemed to feel Percy was her exclusive property and kept warning the other to back off."

"I don't think—"

"That's when I decided it was time to get out of there. I figured now that Mother knew what kind of man she was dealing with, she'd have the good sense to dump the guy."

I shook my head in amazement.

"What?" He looked mystified.

"I can't believe you didn't stay around and see who won the . . . discussion."

"Look, I was tired, okay? I headed back to the cabin and—to save you the trouble of asking—I watched TV. Alone. Until about eleven. Then I went to bed." His jaw tightened, daring me to challenge his alibi. When I didn't, he went on to add, "Don't you think I've gone over that night a million times in my head? What if I'd stayed? Maybe there was something I could've done to prevent what happened."

I took pity on him. "There's no way you could've known what was going to happen that night."

His eyes glistened with unshed tears. "Every time I go by the house, I keep expecting my mother to come waltzing into the room, ready to read me the riot act for not measuring up to her high standards."

"I'm sorry for your loss." Even though Camilla wasn't always likable, she was part of our community. I thought it only fitting to observe a moment of silence in her honor. That accomplished, I decided it was time to hightail it back to the garden center before I bumped into Jolene.

As it happened, I may have cut my departure a little close. As I was pulling out of the parking lot, Jolene was pulling in. But, hey, she barreled past me so fast, my face was probably nothing more than a blur.

And if Keith had the good sense to keep his mouth shut, she'd never even know I'd been there.

CHAPTER TWENTY-SEVEN

A driving need to fit all the pieces together propelled me back to the scene of the crime. Tony answered the door dressed in tan slacks and a blue cotton shirt. There were bags under his eyes, as if he hadn't been sleeping well. His reaction to my presence mimicked his brother's: the welcoming smile vanished the moment he realized who was standing on his doorstep.

"What do you want?" he demanded.

From the way he was acting, Evelyn must've clued him in that I'd been digging into their financial affairs. Slipping into my friendly neighbor, just-stopping-by-to-say-hello routine, I said, "I just came by to see how you were holding up." Not trusting in my own acting ability, which certainly wasn't on par with Happy and Lula Mae's, I brushed past him before he had time to come up with an excuse to get rid of me.

I had to hand it to him, he handled the situation with more grace than I would have. "I was getting ready to have a glass of lemonade," he said. "Care to join me?"

Flashing him my best smile, I said, "I'd love to."

He bypassed the living room, which probably held too many unpleasant memories, and led me to a room along the back. Walls of glass surrounded us on three sides, providing a perfect home for all those plants Camilla had purchased before her death. Plants which, now that I had a chance to observe them, weren't looking so good.

"These plants"—I made a sweeping gesture with my hand—

"need water. Do you have a watering can anywhere?"

He shrugged. "I have no idea."

"Well, you need to get one. We have some down at the Flower Patch. If you like, I can bring one by. In the meantime, if you have a water pitcher, I could—"

"I'm not really a plant person," he said. "Maybe I should donate them to a nursing home, or something."

Remembering my promise to Mrs. Cobb about donating plants to the old folks' place, I offered to take them off his hands. He agreed, and we spent a few minutes hauling them out to my truck. "Now for that lemonade I promised you," he said as we returned to the sunroom.

While I settled down on the white rattan sofa with lemon-yellow cushions, he squirmed around in one of the matching chairs, looking uncomfortable. "Evelyn had some shopping to do in town, but she should be back soon."

Falling back on the manners Happy had drilled into my brain from youth, I said, "I'm sorry for not calling before dropping by. It was very inconsiderate of me."

"No apology needed. I wasn't doing anything important, just wandering around the house, looking at all the stuff Mother's collected over the years. I have no idea what we're going to do with it." He reached for the pitcher of lemonade sitting on the coffee table, filled two glasses, then handed one to me.

"You could always have an estate sale," I suggested.

"Maybe." He didn't sound enthused by the idea.

I took a sip of lemonade, decided it was too sweet for my taste, and returned it to the table. "Have you decided what you're going to do with the house?"

"Why? You interested in buying it?"

I met his gaze. "Not me, but I have a friend who's looking for a place."

He leaned back, rested his hands along the arms of the chair.

"Well, Mother did leave the house to me and Keith but I have—"

"—a business to run back in Houston."

He studied me a moment. "If it were just me . . . but Evelyn, she's not used to small towns. Even if I did want to stay, like you said, I have a business to run. There's no way I could just pick up and move. And Keith has a good job in New York, so I'm sure he won't want the place."

"The house is in good shape. You should get a good price for it, which should keep the wolves at bay for a while."

His sharp blue eyes rested on me. "Evelyn mentioned that you'd heard some of the rumors floating around about Davenport Hardware. I hope you're not one of those people who believe everything they hear."

I shrugged.

"Think about it," he said. "With the economy in such a slump, more people are choosing to stay put. That means building on, remodeling—"

I got the picture. "Which means more business for you." Not willing to let him off the hook so easily, I said, "The funny thing is, I find most rumors usually have a kernel of truth at their core."

He gave me a measuring look. "That's probably true in some cases, but, I assure you, Davenport Hardware is rock solid."

"Even with all the big chains cutting into your business?"

His jaw tightened. "Chain stores can't offer customers the personal service we provide. All our sales associates are very knowledgeable about the building trades. They can accurately estimate the cost of a project, assist in gathering the needed materials, as well as offer tips on how to complete the project."

"I see." A moment passed. Then, keeping my tone light, as if his answer didn't really matter, I said, "I suppose you and Evelyn were in Houston when you heard the news about your mother's death."

His eyes narrowed. "Is this your way of asking if Evelyn and I have alibis for the night Mother was killed?"

"Well, you have to admit, you and Keith have the most to gain by your mother's death."

His nostrils flared. He busied himself pouring another glass of lemonade. Abandoned it on the table without taking a sip. "If it will get you off my back." His gaze locked with mine. "I'll be happy to tell you where we were that night."

He waited for my nod of agreement before proceeding. "Evelyn was at the Riverside Inn in New Orleans attending her college roommate's wedding. From what I'm told, the reception lasted well into the night. And since I didn't have any reason to hurry home, I stayed late at the store, caught up on some paperwork. Trust me, if I'd known I was going to need an alibi, I would've had one of my employees stick around."

"I don't suppose you stopped for a pizza on your way home, or ran into a neighbor when you picked up the newspaper."

"Afraid not. But there's no way I could get to Port Springs and be back in time for work the next morning. Which I was. And on time."

"Unless you flew."

"Which I didn't."

I studied him, trying to decide if he was being truthful.

"Look, the police have checked all this out," he said. "If there were any inconsistencies in our stories, I'm sure they would have discovered them by now."

He had a point. "Still, you and your brother have the most to gain by your mother's death."

"Money-wise, yes. But whoever killed Mother could've wanted her out of the way for some other reason."

I knew where he was headed with this line of thinking. "My aunt is a sweet, generous, old woman. She's not a killer."

"And I'm supposed to take your word for that."

This was getting us nowhere. Evelyn would be home soon, then it would be two against one. Time to get moving.

Too late. As I stood up to leave, Evelyn barreled into the room loaded down with packages. "I could use some help here," she said to Tony.

As if he'd been caught in a compromising position, Tony bounced to his feet. "Honey, you remember Kate Spencer, don't you?" He grabbed an armful of packages from her. "She stopped by to see what we planned on doing about the house."

"Really." Evelyn dumped her purse and the remaining packages into an empty chair. "I didn't realize you were in the real-estate business."

"I'm not," I told her, "but I know someone's who's looking for a place. That is, if you're interested in selling?"

She plopped down on the sofa I'd vacated and slipped off her shoes. "I guess we'll have to give it some thought. In the meantime, maybe you could do us a favor."

I had an uneasy feeling in my gut. "What would that be?"

She smiled slyly. "You can tell us who killed my mother-in-law."

"How should I know?"

"Seems to me you know pretty much everything that's going on in this town."

I decided the wisest course of action would be to skedaddle. "Well, I'd love to stay and chat, but I really have to get back to work."

Evelyn smiled. "There's no need to rush off on my account. Stay and have lunch with us. I'm sure Pricilla can whip up something scrumptious for us to eat. And while we're eating, you can fill us in on what the police are doing to catch my mother-in-law's killer."

"What makes you think I know what the police are doing? I get my news from the media, same as everyone else."

"Oh, come on now. You don't expect us to believe that." Her green eyes had a knowing quality that I found downright insulting. "The way I hear it, that boyfriend of yours is in charge of the investigation."

I quickly set her straight about my relationship to Steven.

"Really. Rumor has it that you two used to be pretty tight. Were even engaged at one time. That could explain why that aunt of yours isn't sitting in jail right now."

I could feel the vein in my temple begin to throb. "My aunt isn't in jail because she hasn't done anything wrong."

Evelyn tilted her head to one side and gave me an icy stare. "And those earrings the police found in your aunt's car, they didn't really belong to Camilla. They belonged to . . . some other dead woman."

I managed to hang on to my temper. Just barely. "If you will excuse me, I need to get back to the garden center. Tony, you can let me know what you plan on doing about the house."

"I'll do that." Sounding relieved, he hustled me from the room before Evelyn had time to object. When we reached the front door, he said, "If I were you, I wouldn't come nosing around here again." Then he nudged me through the opening and slammed the door in my face.

As I was backing out of the driveway, there came a loud honk, then a silver Lexus whipped past me and jerked to a stop. Careening out of the vehicle, Keith barreled around my truck to the driver's side. This was all I needed. I let out a sigh, then rolled down the window.

"Had any luck bullying a confession out of my brother? Or am I still your number one suspect?"

"For your information, I was just being neighborly."

He took a step forward, "Yeah, right." He looked ready to strangle me.

Deciding not to give him the chance, I slammed the truck

into reverse and shot out of the drive. Missed crushing his foot by mere inches.

On the drive home, pesky details began to rattle around in my brain. Like, Percy's car was abandoned out by the lake. Was it possible Keith hired Percy to steal his mother's jewelry? Then something went wrong. Percy panicked. Killed Camilla. Leaving Keith no choice but to help Percy disappear?

And what about Tony's financial problems? How serious were they? His alibi was certainly shaky.

I banged my hand on the steering wheel in frustration. What I needed were answers. Not more questions.

A big piece of this maze-without-end had to do with Percy. If I could find him, maybe I could figure out who killed Camilla and our lives could get back to normal. This was a small town. Percy couldn't have gone far without wheels. If I were Percy, where would I hide? It would have to be someplace nearby. Someplace where I felt safe.

Then it hit me. What better place to hide than Lula Mae's house. Everyone in town knew she was staying at our place until this murder situation was resolved. I glanced at my watch. There wasn't time to check out my theory now; after all, I still had a business to run, but I'd definitely drop by her place in the very near future.

CHAPTER TWENTY-EIGHT

To say Happy was relieved to see me when I lumbered into the office some ten minutes later is definitely an understatement. "Where have you been?" she said. "This place has been an absolute madhouse. Jolene took off for some fancy lunch, and you were nowhere to be found. I've a good mind to pack my things and head to Florida. Spend the few remaining years I have left lying on the beach, basking in the sunshine."

"You don't like sand," I reminded her. "And sunshine is bad for your complexion."

"I can learn to like sand." Her mouth was set in a definite pout. "And haven't you heard? Sunshine is good for the bones. It supplies vitamin D."

"Why don't you go on home and get some rest?" I suggested. "Jolene will be back soon. I can handle things until then."

For once in her life she didn't argue or complain that I was treating her like some washed-up old woman. I guess the tension of the last few days was finally getting to her.

She wasn't exaggerating about the place being busy. I hardly had time to catch my breath between customers. And to make matters worse, it was nearly closing time before Jolene showed up. "That was a lousy thing to do," she lit into me.

So, Keith had ratted me out. "You're right." I ignored the old man waving for help by the fruit trees. "I don't know what got into me. There's no excuse for my behavior." I made a play for her sympathy. "It's just that . . . I guess this thing with Lula

Mae is making me a little crazy."

I could sense the struggle going on inside her. On one hand, she was awfully fond of Lula Mae; yet, at the same time, she probably felt her loyalty belonged to Keith. "Okay," she said, accepting my apology. "But from now on you'd better not—"

"Don't worry." I held up my hand to forestall her lecture. "I've learned my lesson. I promise never to interfere in your love life again." I made a motion across my chest. "Cross my heart and hope to die."

Her eyes narrowed. "If it ever happens again, I'll find myself another job. Someplace where the boss doesn't stick her nose into my personal life."

"It won't happen again," I promised. And hoped I wasn't telling a lie.

That evening Happy and Lula Mae were camped out in the living room when I came downstairs for my date with Steven. Noticing my attire, a simple, rose-colored sundress, their mouths dropped open in unison.

I bristled. It was not as if they'd never seen me in anything but jeans.

Happy looked puzzled. "Is today some holiday we've forgotten about?"

I busied myself straightening magazines. "Not that I know of."

Her eyes narrowed to reptilian slits. "Then why the dress?"

"Not that it's any of your business," I said, "but a friend happens to be picking me up. We're going out for a bite to eat."

"How nice," Lula Mae said. "You haven't been out in ages. The fresh air will do you good."

"It's not like I'm a hermit," I said.

"I've been telling your mother," she went on, "that you spend way too much time with us old folks. You'll never catch a

husband that way. You have to get out there and circulate. Do
. . . whatever people your age do these days."

"It may come as a shock to you," I said, feeling a little miffed,
"but people my age do the same thing as people your age do.
Go to movies. Go out to eat. Hang out at the beach."

"Well, I don't know about hanging out at the beach. My
skin's way too delicate for that. But eating out—that's something
I'm quite good at." She regarded me thoughtfully. "You might
like to try that new restaurant downtown. Tommy's Kitchen, I
think it's called. The food's pretty good."

Happy couldn't stay on the sidelines a moment longer.
Launching in to investigative mode, she said, "It seems strange
that you haven't mentioned anything about going out before
now."

There was no getting around it. Happy would badger me
until she ferreted out every detail of my plans. Even if it took all
night. "The fact is," I said, "I have a date. Surely, you remember
what those are."

"Of course, I remember. I'm just surprised that you do."

Lula Mae smiled benevolently. "Are you going out with that
nice young man down at Barney's Motors? He's right nice looking, if you ask me."

"Since when do you go out on dates?" Happy couldn't let it
go.

I threw up my hands as if to ward off a blow. "It's not as if I
never go out. Just last"—I had to think for a moment—"January, I went out with that insurance salesman."

"And you remember what a disaster that was," Happy said.

"It wasn't that bad."

She folded her hands across her chest and glared at me. "He
tried to sell you a life insurance policy."

"Okay, so it was pretty bad."

Easing over to the window, I peeked outside. No Steven in

sight. Letting the curtain fall gently into place, I turned around to find two sets of eyes regarding me with suspicion.

"Okay." I gave up any right to privacy. "I'm going out to dinner with Steven Griggs. Satisfied?"

"That young man who arrested me?" Lula Mae sounded horrified.

"He didn't arrest you; he only questioned you. Besides, he's a cop. It's his job to question people. He had no choice in the matter."

"Oh, he had a choice, all right," Happy said. "The man's known Lula Mae since he was in diapers. He knows she'd never kill anyone. When I think what that man did to—"

I cut her off. "It's not Steven's fault Lula Mae was engaged to that Romeo who was trying to con half the women in town out of their life's savings."

The choked sounds coming from Lula Mae's throat alerted me to the danger I'd stepped into. "Sorry, Lula Mae. I didn't mean that the way it sounded."

Out came a wad of tissues. "I should hope not."

Family loyalty saturated Happy's very pores. "Your young man had no right to put Lula Mae through such a terrible ordeal."

"How many times do I have to tell you? Steven is not my young man. We're just having dinner, not eloping."

"Have you forgotten what happened the last time you two got together?" Happy asked. "I never bought into that cold-feet business. He must've done something pretty awful to make you run away like that."

My ears caught the sound of an engine. Snatching my purse off the coffee table, I ran for the door. Steven, dressed in a pair of khaki pants and a blue plaid shirt, was coming up the walk as I barreled down the front steps.

"It's customary to wait for your date to—" he began.

160

"Unless you want to sit through one of Happy's lectures, I suggest you get moving."

The man wasn't stupid. He pivoted around and double-timed it back to his truck, a shiny black affair, complete with a stainless steel toolbox in the bed. We were out of the driveway and halfway down the block before I calmed down enough to speak. "You have no idea how lucky you are."

He glanced my way. "Who do you think took the flak when you left town all those years ago?"

Okay, so maybe he did know. "How bad was it?"

"Let's just say Attila the Hun couldn't have done a better job."

CHAPTER TWENTY-NINE

As we drove along the familiar roads, Steven and I lapsed into silence, each wrapped in our own thoughts. We hit the highway and headed west. The sudden glare of sunlight in my eyes blinded me. Wishing I had thought to bring my sunglasses, I reached up and flipped down the visor.

In the air-conditioned interior of Steven's truck the woodsy scent of his cologne mingled with my lighter scent. For some reason I couldn't decide what to do with my hands. I finally settled on folding them in my lap.

"Your dad came by the Flower Patch last week and bought a couple of pear trees, a fig tree, and about a dozen blueberry bushes."

"Sounds like he's turning into a regular farmer," Steven said with a note of pride in his voice.

I made a mental note to speak with Happy about offering edible landscaping classes. "I hope he realizes how much space that many plants will take."

"I wouldn't worry about it. Dad inherited my grandmother's place."

A picture flashed through my mind of a tiny old woman with warm hands and a gentle smile. "I haven't been by your grandmother's place in ages."

"Grandma Hall was some woman. Every year she'd send us boys out to the railroad tracks to pick dewberries. Man, was it tiring work. But those cobblers were well worth it."

"Amen to that." I, too, had spent many hours picking dewberries. Except for stumbling across an occasional snake, I hadn't minded the work. And those cobblers, warm from the oven, their crusts so tender and sweet . . . I was beginning to salivate just thinking about them. "Happy's always telling me the way to a man's heart is through his stomach. I guess she's right."

"There are other ways."

I was not about to go there. "How's your brother doing?"

He chuckled. "Mike's doing fine. As a matter of fact, he and Rose are expecting their second child any day now." He began to fill me in on the latest antics of Lori, Mike and Rose's firstborn.

As we crossed the bridge, I noticed the strip of beach to our left was still dotted with sun worshipers taking advantage of the last rays of light. We drove on for several minutes, then turned into the parking lot of what had once been a seafood processing plant, but now housed a restaurant with several small tourist shops along one side.

Inside the restaurant, ceiling fans whirred overhead. Crab pots, oyster rakes, and other items used in the seafood industry were tacked to the walls. A woman in a bright red outfit led us to a table overlooking the Gulf.

As we perused the menu, I noticed Steven staring at me. "What?"

He tossed his menu on the table. "It's been a long time since I've seen you smile like that."

I sighed. "It's a wonder I remember how. Especially with all that's been going on."

"You need to take some time to relax, have some fun, or you're going to burn out."

"You're one to talk," I said.

"What's that supposed to mean?"

"Everyone knows cops are prone to burnout. I was reading

this book a few weeks ago written by a police psychologist about how stress affects the lives of cops and their families. Believe me, she didn't paint a pretty picture."

Before he could respond, the waitress came to take our order. Everything sounded so good. I had a hard time deciding what to order. I finally made my decision, then settled back in my seat, willing myself to relax.

After the waitress took Steven's order, we chatted a few minutes about some of the items used in the seafood industry, which were displayed on the walls. That dredged up old memories. "Remember all those times we took your dad's boat out to the barrier islands?" I said.

"I remember a little pink bathing suit you were very fond of."

"I seem to recall you were pretty fond of it yourself."

He gave me a quick once-over. "You've filled out a bit since then."

"Fattened up, you mean."

"Contrary to what Hollywood thinks, most men want a woman with some meat on their bones."

"Just not too much."

He was saved from answering by the arrival of our food: steaming bowls of seafood gumbo served with fluffy white rice and chunks of crusty French bread, perfect for dipping. We both made a grab for the hot sauce. He relinquished his grip on the bottle. "Ladies first."

"Aren't you the gentleman." I gave my food a good splash of the spicy hot sauce, then handed him the bottle.

"I try to be." He gave his own food a hefty dash.

"Not as good as Happy's," I critiqued the food, "but not bad."

He agreed with my assessment. "I doubt many professional chefs could dish up better food than your mother."

How we always managed to return to the subject of food was

a mystery to me.

Once we'd filled our bellies, we bypassed the tourist shops in favor of a stroll along the beach. Battling the sand, which continually filled our shoes, was a no-win situation. Finally, we did the only sensible thing—slipped off our shoes and carried them.

We moved to the water's edge where the sand was hard packed, which made walking easier. Gentle waves rolled into shore providing soothing background music. "How much trouble is Lula Mae really in?" I asked, after we had walked a good piece down the beach.

He sighed. "It doesn't look good. The long-standing feud between the two women is bad enough. Add to that, Lula Mae was seen going into Camilla's house around the time of the murder. Truth is, I'm going out on a limb for not hauling her back down to the station for more questioning."

"You know as well as I do, Lula Mae wouldn't kill anyone. Remember our high-school biology class?"

"How could I forget? I thought Mrs. Calloway was going to have a heart attack when Lula Mae marched into her classroom with her 'save the frogs' sign."

We laughed.

I had forgotten how nice his laugh was. Reaching out an arm, he pulled me to him. When his lips came down gently on mine, I forgot all about Lula Mae and her problems. I was lost in the moment, caught up in a whirlwind of feelings that I thought were buried so deeply they'd never resurface.

"I've wanted to do that all evening," Steven said when we broke apart.

The look in his eyes sent fingers of panic stirring. Jolting back to earth, I searched for an avenue of escape. Then did the one thing I promised myself I wouldn't do—I handed him the notebook I'd stashed in my purse for safekeeping.

"What's this?" Steven asked.

"Take a look."

He threw me a puzzled look, but did as I asked and flipped through the pages. Then he stopped, went back to the beginning, and began to read more carefully. "Where did you get this?"

"Uh . . ." I should have anticipated the question.

"Please don't tell me you were snooping again?"

My backbone stiffened. "I do not snoop."

"Okay." He held up a hand. "Please don't tell me you were . . . investigating . . . again."

"Since you put it so nicely," I said, somewhat appeased, "I came across it while inspecting Percy's closet."

"And you were inspecting Percy's closet because . . . ?" He waited for a response.

I couldn't very well tell him the truth: we were looking for clues to his whereabouts. "Uh, we dropped by to see if any of his plants needed watering, or the fridge needed cleaning out. Nothing important."

"So you weren't ransacking the place, looking for all the stuff he stole from Lula Mae?"

I glanced down at my feet, where rose-colored nails stood out against the white sand. "That too," I admitted, my voice so low he probably had to strain to hear it.

"If I'm not mistaken, Joe confiscated Lula Mae's key when he caught them snooping around Percy's place a few days ago. So how did you get in?"

I'd forgotten about that. "Uh . . ." My mind raced for a plausible explanation.

Treating me like some cornered suspect, he waited silently, giving me plenty of time to squirm.

"Okay," I finally said. "Percy kept a spare key under the front porch. We used it to get inside." I paused a moment, then added,

"You know as well as I do, the man has to know something about Camilla's death. He was having dinner with her the night she was killed. He either saw who killed her or did the deed himself."

He played along. "What's his motive for killing her?"

I'd given it a lot of thought over the past few days. "Camilla found out about all the other women he was seeing, realized he was using her, and threatened to expose him."

"Possible," he conceded.

More scenarios played through my mind. "Or maybe she caught him with his hand in her jewelry box. Or realized he was planning to bilk her out of money for a business he had no intention of starting. Or maybe—"

He held up a hand. "I suppose, it never occurred to the three of you that you might be putting your lives in danger."

My temper started to rise. "We were just checking out Percy's house, not hanging out in some back alley."

"And Camilla Davenport was just having dinner in her own home."

My chin tilted up in defiance. "There were three of us."

He crossed his arms and glared at me. "A lot of difference that would make against a gun."

"I know how to dial 9-1-1."

He arched his brows. "From that cell phone of yours?"

"Okay, you win. It was dumb of us to go over there with a killer on the loose."

He tucked the notebook into the pocket of his pants. "Maybe we should talk about something else."

I felt my shoulders relax. "Like?"

He smiled. "Like, where we're going on our next date?"

I wasn't sure there was going to be a next date. I glanced around, spotted one of the swing sets that were scattered along this part of the beach, and sprinted toward it.

Steven caught up with me in seconds. "Why is it that every time we start to talk about anything more personal than the weather, you go running off like a frightened rabbit?"

Dumping my shoes on the ground, I slid into one of the black rubber swings and dangled my feet in the cooling sand. "Probably because I feel like a frightened rabbit whenever you're around."

He stepped in front of me and grabbed the stainless steel chains. Streetlights from the nearby highway flicked on. "Don't you think it's time you faced up to your fear?"

Leaning back, I stared up at the sky, searching for the first star of the night. The wishing star, Happy called it. When I located it, I closed my eyes and wished for the courage to trust the man standing before me.

After a moment, I opened my eyes and looked up at him. "I'm trying," I said softly.

He moved around behind me and gave the swing a hard push. "Try harder," he said, as I sailed high into the air.

CHAPTER THIRTY

The next morning, I breezed into the kitchen to find Happy and Lula Mae devouring stacks of blueberry pancakes, along with crisp slices of bacon. Both had on faded robes and their hair stuck out in tufts as if they had just stepped off a roller coaster.

Dressed in my best satin pajamas, I felt like a fairy princess. "Isn't it a glorious day?" I reached into the fridge for a carton of orange juice.

Both women stopped eating and turned to stare at me. "What's so glorious about it?" Happy demanded.

"Well . . ." I leaned over the sink and looked out the window. "The sun's shining, the flowers are blooming, and the squirrels are chattering up a storm."

There came a collective groan from the vicinity of the table.

I swung around. "What's wrong with you two?"

"You," Happy said. "You're what's wrong with us."

"Me. What did I do?"

"For starters, you're prancing around here sounding like some lovesick pup," Happy said.

"Can't I appreciate what a gorgeous day it is without you jumping to conclusions?"

Happy was getting steamed. "I can't believe you actually went out with that man after the way he treated Lula Mae."

"He's certainly no gentleman, that's for sure," Lula Mae agreed, getting into the spirit of things. "In my day, a young man came inside and visited with a girl's family before he took her out."

"The man's name is Steven Griggs," I reminded them. "And you both should be ashamed of yourselves for slandering the name of such an upstanding member of society. A man who risks his life every day to keep the streets safe for this community."

Happy turned a bright shade of pink. And for once she seemed to have run out of words.

"Besides," I continued my tirade, "on more than one occasion, I've heard both of you say what a good family he comes from."

"His mother was on our bowling league last year," Happy grudgingly admitted.

Picking up on Happy's change of attitude, Lula Mae added, "And his father is one of the deacons down at Community Fellowship Church."

Not ready to give in so easily, Happy said, "But Lula Mae is right about one thing. A proper young man would come inside and visit with a girl's family before taking her gallivanting around town."

I made a noise somewhere between a yell and a growl.

"Hang on to your britches," Happy said. "We get the message. Now take that stack of pancakes I have warming for you out of the oven and eat your breakfast. If you wait much longer, they'll be so hard you'll crack a tooth on them and have to spend all morning at the dentist."

Happy and Lula Mae had another cup of coffee while I devoured the stack of blueberry pancakes they'd saved me, which I topped with a generous serving of yummy maple syrup. The real stuff, not that imitation kind, which Happy would never allow within a hundred yards of her kitchen.

"By the way, we checked out those phone calls Percy made to

Mobile," Happy said. "Seems he's been calling a diner. A place called Mulberry's."

"We had lunch there," Lula Mae said. "That Jonah, he makes a pretty good meatloaf."

Happy eyed me suspiciously. "He told us some woman had already been by the place looking for her uncle."

"Really." I attacked my pancakes with more gusto.

"Funny thing is," Happy went on, "the woman he described sounded a lot like you."

I shook my head. "He must've been mistaken."

"He told us her name was Kate and that she was looking for her Uncle Percy. Seems her mother was worried about him because he'd missed some wedding."

"Okay." I took a sip of milk. "So I was there. Big deal."

Happy crossed her arms and glared at me. "I thought you said we were in this together."

"I didn't see how Jonah could have anything to do with Camilla's murder. He's not even from around here."

"How about Mrs. Mayfield?" Happy said. "You think she had anything to do with Camilla's death?"

"She's a nice old woman. She wouldn't kill a spider."

"Our thoughts exactly," Happy agreed.

I glanced at her in surprise. "You met Mrs. Mayfield?"

"Of course we did. The two of us"—she glanced at Lula Mae—"happen to be very good at this investigating business."

Thinking about all the trouble they could've gotten themselves into put a damper on my appetite. I got up and scraped the rest of my breakfast into the trash can. "Next time you two decide to play detectives," I said, "how about giving me a call. I'd be happy to drive you where you need to go."

"And vice versa," Happy said. "The part about calling us if you decide to investigate," she amended.

"Yeah," Lula Mae piped up, "don't go running off without us

again. Happy and I have a knack for getting people to talk. You'd be surprised at all the secrets we're able to weasel out of people."

I arched my brows. "Such as?"

"Uh, well." She shot a panicked look in Happy's direction.

"Like Mrs. Mayfield's husband owned the diner outright," Happy said. "And the house she lives in is paid for. He also had a small life insurance policy and a few CDs."

"None of that has anything to do with Camilla's death."

"Maybe not," Happy said. "But it does prove we're still useful. Not some washed-up old women, who can't—"

"I get the point." Loud and clear. "We're in this together."

The rest of the day passed in a blur of activities. At church, several people commented about how cheerful I seemed. What, was I some kind of grouch before? Later, the three of us spent a leisurely afternoon playing board games and feeding our faces with all that scrumptious food left over from Happy's baking spree.

When Happy and Lula Mae finally trundled upstairs for a nap, I grabbed my keys off the table and headed for Lucille's place, hoping to get a line on her houseguest.

Like any good detective, I drove by and cased the joint first. Noted: her car was in the driveway, and the drapes closed up tight. I continued to the end of the road, turned around, then eased to a stop four houses down from my target.

As a disguise, I jammed on a baseball cap, then climbed out and started walking. Once I hit the edge of her property, I abandoned power-walking speed for stroll mode. As far as I could tell, there wasn't so much as a crack between any of the drapes.

This situation called for drastic action. Action that I hoped none of her neighbors would notice and go calling the police about. After checking to be sure the coast was clear, I sprinted down the driveway and slid around back.

On this side of the house, most of the drapes were open. I hugged the wall and took a quick peek through the first window. A bedroom, filled with antique furniture, done in calming shades of green. But the lack of paraphernalia on the dresser suggested no recent occupant.

I moved over to the next window. From its smaller size—a bathroom, I guessed. It was shut up tighter than a coffin.

At the third window, my luck changed. It was partially open, its curtains billowing in the breeze. A quick glance confirmed it was occupied. Thankful for the wooden fence, which surrounded the backyard and protected it from nosy neighbors, I hunkered down and tuned in on the conversation going on inside.

"Oh dear," I heard Lucille say, "what do you plan to do now?"

I waited for an answer to her question. When none was forthcoming, I risked another look inside. Saw Lucille, seated at the kitchen table, the phone glued to her ear.

After ten minutes of listening to her mindless chatter, my back started to ache. I squirmed around, trying to find a comfortable position. Finally, I gave up and plopped down on the ground. A gentle breeze began to caress my skin. Soon my eyelids started to grow heavy.

The next thing I knew, someone was jabbing a hole in my shoulder. My eyes flew open. Without thinking, I flung up a hand to defend myself. And connected with an arm. A bony arm that happened to be attached to . . . my mother.

Happy swatted me. "What are you trying to do, knock my arm off?" she whispered.

My brain shifted into gear. "What are you doing here?" I snapped back.

"Same thing you're doing here," she said. "Looking for Percy."

"How did you know where I was?"

She rolled her eyes. "We saw your truck parked down the block, genius."

Lula Mae shoved her way between us. "Did we miss anything?" she asked, keeping her voice low. "Has Percy been hiding out at Lucille's?"

I struggled to my feet, trying to work the kinks out of my body without alerting Lucille to our presence. "I'm not sure."

"Hang on a minute," we heard Lucille say. "I think I hear something outside."

The three of us shut up and hunkered beneath the window.

There was a brief pause in the conversation, then she said, "Never mind. It must have been the neighbor's cat."

I motioned for Happy and Lula Mae to follow me. They trailed behind me to the front sidewalk. "This spying in the window business is getting us nowhere," I said.

Happy snorted. "You don't say."

"What we need is a plan," I told them. "Some excuse to get inside and snoop around. Got any brilliant ideas?"

"We have one of Happy's apple pies in the car," Lula Mae said, trying to be helpful.

I glanced at Happy. She shrugged. "Like you said, we needed an excuse to get inside."

Why was I surprised? In Happy's book, food was the solution to every problem.

We hoofed it down the street to the Blue Bomber, which was parked behind my truck, and drove the short distance back to Lucille's. She answered the door dressed in a bright yellow dress, and didn't look pleased to see us. "I was just on my way out," she told us.

"This won't take but a minute." Not waiting for an invitation, Happy barged inside. "I brought you one of my apple pies. I know how much you love them. If you're really nice, I might even tell you my secret ingredient."

Lucille held onto the door, looking flustered. "But I was—"

"Where are your manners, Lucille?" Lula Mae nudged past her friend. "Like Happy said, we brought you one of her apple pies." Keeping my mouth shut, I shuffled along in Lula Mae's wake as she kept up a stream of small talk.

"I'll just put this pie in the kitchen," Happy called out, then sailed off before Lucille could object.

Lula Mae and I did our parts. We corralled Lucille in the living room and kept her talking. "How's that sweet little nephew of yours doing?" Lula Mae asked, plopping down beside me on the sofa.

Looking uneasy, Lucille perched on the edge of her chair. "I haven't seen him since Christmas, when he and his mama spent the week with me. Why?"

Lula Mae flashed her a smile. "Well, it seems that my niece here is interested in finding herself a husband."

"What?" my voice came out a croak.

"She's been dating some policeman, but Happy and I don't think he's a suitable match for our little girl," Lula Mae went on. "I seem to recall that your nephew is single. And he's a doctor, isn't that right?"

"Just a minute," I said. "I am not in the market for a husband."

Lula Mae ignored me. "You think you could invite Melvin for dinner some night so he and Kate can get acquainted?"

I had met Melvin on several occasions. And I don't care if he is a doctor, I am not—I repeat, am not—interested in the man. "I already have a boyfriend," I blurted out, hoping to put an end to her scheming.

Lula Mae studied me with those big brown eyes of hers. "If I'm not mistaken, dear, you told us that young man was not your boyfriend."

"She's right," Happy said, joining us. "You did say that.

175

Several times, in fact."

I felt my temper start to rise. "What is this? A conspiracy to get me married off?"

"There's no need to get huffy, young lady," Happy said. "We're just looking out for your welfare." She eased down beside Lula Mae on the sofa. "Oh, Lucille, I noticed a man's shaving kit by the sink when I used the bathroom just now. Are you sure your nephew hasn't been staying with you?"

A touch of panic slid across Lucille's face. "How stupid of me," she said quickly. "I remember now. Melvin was here last week. He must have forgotten to pack his shaving kit when he left." Then, as if the idea suddenly popped into her head, she added, "Maybe Kate can join us for dinner when he drives down to pick it up."

Not in this lifetime. "Thank you for the invitation," I said, "but we're pretty busy at the garden center this time of year."

"Well, we don't want to hold you up any longer." Happy shot to her feet. Lula Mae and I followed her lead. As we were filing out the door, Happy turned around. "By the way, you haven't heard from Percy, have you?"

Lucille looked as if she might fall over in a dead faint. To hold herself up, she leaned against the door frame. "I'm sure the man's long gone by now."

"Last I heard, he had no vehicle to get out of town in," I said.

Lucille frowned. "He must have arranged for other transportation."

"You think Percy actually whacked Camilla?" Happy asked.

What was with this "whacked" business?

Lucille's chocolate-brown eyes narrowed. "I most certainly do not. Percy may be many things, but he's not a killer."

Lula Mae huffed out her shoulders. "You sound like you're still sweet on the man."

"Don't be silly, Lula Mae. If you remember, I'm the one who came down to the garden center to warn you about him."

"Yeah." Lula Mae folded her arms across her chest. "And now I'm beginning to wonder why you did that."

"Oh, for goodness sakes. I have no designs on the man. You can have him if you want him. Though why you'd want him beats me."

Lula Mae's body puffed up like a riled bear. "For your information, I'm not interested in Percy Moss. He's nothing but a thief and a liar." Flinging her purse over one shoulder, she flounced down the steps and piled into the car.

Happy and I lingered on the front porch. "If Percy's such a loser, why are you letting him stay here?" I asked.

Lucille's face flamed. "Like I told your mother," she said, steam practically billowing from her nostrils, "there's nobody here but me." Abandoning manners, she spun around and stomped back inside, slamming the door so hard she rattled the nearby windows.

CHAPTER THIRTY-ONE

Monday morning arrived too soon. Several hours after we opened the Flower Patch, I found myself cramming azalea bushes into Mrs. Cobb's trunk. "That should do it," I said.

"Are you sure your foot's all right?" she asked.

"It's fine." To demonstrate, I wiggled the foot in question up and down several times, and tried not to wince as a streak of pain shot up my leg.

"I don't know what got into me. I'm usually not so clumsy. But that angel statue . . . it seemed to topple over all by itself."

I plastered on a smile. "No harm done."

"I must say, you're in a good mood today."

"That's because it's such a beautiful day."

"It was a beautiful day last week when I was in here, but I don't remember you being so bright-eyed and cheerful then."

A familiar black truck swept into the parking lot, sending my heart beating in double-time. When Steven climbed out of his truck, Mrs. Cobb smiled. "I hope you're not here about that parking ticket I got last week."

"No, ma'am. My business here is strictly personal."

"Hmm." Mrs. Cobb's eyes showed a spark of interest.

I knew I should be upset with him. By this time tomorrow the entire town would be speculating about our relationship. But for some unfathomable reason, I couldn't bring myself to care.

Steven looked at me. "I thought I'd see if you were free for lunch."

Even though Mrs. Cobb was watching us, I grinned like someone who had won the lottery. Our audience expanded when Happy and Lula Mae came tearing out of the office. "You were supposed to be helping Mrs. Cobb load her plants," Happy said, shooting me an accusing look, "not lollygagging in the parking lot."

I nodded toward the trunk jammed with plants. "All done."

Mrs. Cobb nodded toward Steven. "He came to ask Kate out to lunch."

Happy didn't look pleased. "We have too much to do for you to go gallivanting off someplace."

"Remember the plan," Lula Mae whispered.

"What plan?" I looked back and forth between the two women searching for a clue.

Pursing her lips, Happy refused to answer, so I zeroed in on the weak link. "What plan, Lula Mae?"

Before she could say anything, Happy scooted over and poked her in the side with an elbow. "Ouch. You don't have to break my ribs. I wasn't gonna tell her anything."

I sighed in exasperation.

"Your young man asked you a question," Mrs. Cobb reminded me.

"That I did." Steven arched his brows. "Well?"

Linking my arm with his, I said, "I'd love to have lunch with you," then sailed past the sea of busybodies as if they didn't even exist.

Steven and I sat in his truck several minutes, debating where to go. Since neither of us was eager to be scrutinized by half the town, we settled on a new Chinese place near the highway.

Twenty minutes later, we were seated at a table near the back wall and had placed our order for two beef and broccoli specials.

"About the other night," Steven said, reaching over to take my hand, "I hope you don't think I'm trying to push you into something you're not ready for."

"Maybe I need a little pushing," I admitted. "Truth is: I've been running from my feelings for so long, it's become more of a habit than anything."

"Still, I don't want to force you into something you'll regret."

I gave him the look Happy used on me when she thought I was being less than truthful.

"Okay." He smiled sheepishly. "Maybe that's not entirely true."

I graced him with "the look" again.

"Okay. So maybe I do want to force you to give me a chance. *Us* a chance. Surely you can't blame me for that."

I decided to let him off the hook. "You're not pushing me into anything. I'm a big girl. It's about time I faced my fears and worked through them."

Our food arrived then, and he withdrew his hand. Suddenly starved, I speared a piece of broccoli and popped it into my mouth. Heat seared the roof of my mouth. I grabbed the glass of iced tea beside my plate and quickly downed a few gulps.

"Maybe you should try blowing on your food, or giving it time to cool before you dive in," he suggested.

"What a brilliant idea." My voice dripped with sarcasm.

"Hey, I have lots of brilliant ideas. Want to hear a few more?"

"No thanks."

We attacked our food in silence for several minutes. Then Steven said, "I was thinking I might borrow Dad's boat so we could have a picnic on Horn Island this weekend."

I sighed and set down my fork. "Sounds wonderful. But you realize if this thing with Lula Mae isn't resolved soon, things might get ugly."

"I was afraid you might say that."

I gave him an apologetic look. "Lula Mae's family."

A strange look suddenly crossed his face. My danger alert mechanism kicked into gear. "You aren't going to believe this, but—" he began.

Before he could finish his sentence, a familiar voice interrupted him. "Fancy meeting you two here."

It couldn't be. I swiveled around to find Happy and her trusty sidekick, Lula Mae, grinning at me. "What are you two doing here?"

Happy slapped on an innocent look. "A person has to eat, don't they?"

"Maybe. But they don't have to eat here."

"As you pointed out to me so recently," Happy said, looking smug, "it's a free country."

"Perhaps you ladies would like to join us," Steven suggested, putting an end to our bickering.

"Why, that's very kind of you." Happy promptly plopped down in the chair beside me, leaving Lula Mae to scramble into the empty seat next to Steven.

After the waitress had taken their orders, Lula Mae batted those false eyelashes of hers at Steven and said, "So, have you discovered who murdered Camilla yet?"

Happy conveniently dropped her purse on the floor. As she leaned down to pick it up, she whispered to Lula Mae, "I told you to let me do the talking."

"I was only trying to make conversation," Lula Mae grumbled back.

"So," Happy said, once she'd readjusted herself, "how are your parents doing, Steven?"

He seemed amused. "Last I heard, they were doing just fine."

"That's good." Several seconds ticked by. "And how is that brother of yours? I hear that he and his wife are expecting a new addition to their family any day now."

"That's what the doctor keeps assuring them."

"How nice," Lula Mae said. "I just love babies, don't you, Happy? They're so sweet and cuddly." Happy gave Lula Mae "the look."

Taking the hint, Lula Mae snapped her mouth shut.

"And work," Happy continued. "How are things going on that front?"

"That's enough." I slapped down my napkin.

"What's got you so riled up, dear?" Happy asked. "I was only making polite conversation. If you need to borrow my working medicine, I have a brand new box of laxatives on the bottom shelf in the bathroom."

"Making conversation, my foot. You're trying to badger Steven into telling you about his investigation."

"Just because I have an inquisitive mind—"

"So this is the big plan you two cooked up," I said, "to follow Steven around and pump him for information."

"Don't be ridiculous!" Happy said. "We're just two old ladies having lunch with family and friends."

"Since we're among friends," Steven said, shifting around to face Lula Mae, "I was hoping you could clear something up for me."

Biting her lower lip, Lula Mae looked to Happy for guidance.

Happy's eyes narrowed. "Like what?" she asked suspiciously.

He addressed his question to Lula Mae. "For starters, did Percy ever ask you for money?"

"Certainly not," Lula Mae replied quickly.

"I know you lost your husband recently," he said, advancing into enemy territory. "Did Percy ever show any particular interest in your financial situation? Whether your husband left you a life insurance policy, stocks, anything like that?"

Lula Mae's face grew red. "Well, he did mention that he knew a little something about the stock market and offered to help me pick out a few stocks." She glanced toward Happy, who looked as if she was on the verge of crawling across the table and strangling her baby sister with her own two hands. "But I told him that I couldn't do anything without talking to Happy first," she added quickly.

"You bet your life, you'd better talk to me first. The man could have taken everything George left you to live on and squandered it away in a week."

"Oh, for goodness sakes," Lula Mae grumbled, "I can take care of myself. I don't need you to run interference for me."

For a moment, I thought Happy might explode right then and there. As a precaution, I put a restraining arm around her shoulders. "There's nothing to worry about," I said, in my most soothing voice, "Lula Mae's money is safe."

She wasn't ready to let go. "You didn't let that weasel plunder through your bank records, or any of George's papers, did you?"

"How could he? You have all my important papers at your house. I've haven't even written a check since George died."

"And you never wrote one before George died either," Happy reminded her.

Lula Mae got that hurt-puppy-dog look in her eyes. "I don't understand why everyone thinks I can't take care of myself."

"Probably because you know absolutely nothing about business," Happy said.

"I could learn."

Realizing he'd gotten all he was going to get out of the bickering twosome, Steven said, "Well, this has been loads of fun, but I need to get back to work. Ready to go, Kate?" At my nod, he stood up and tossed a few bills on the table. "Lunch is on me, ladies."

As we headed for the door, I heard Lula Mae say, "I told you this plan of yours would never work."

CHAPTER THIRTY-TWO

The rest of the day passed in a blur of customers. Once we'd finished supper and the dishes were done, I retrieved Lula Mae's spare house key from the junk drawer and grabbed a flashlight. "I'm going out for a while," I called to the twosome watching TV in the living room. Thankfully, they were so engrossed in some crime show that neither one bothered to find out where I was headed.

As I was getting so adept at doing, I parked a block away from Lula Mae's house, then strolled down the sidewalk to her place. After checking to be sure none of her neighbors were skulking about, I sprinted down the driveway and up the front steps.

The streetlight was far enough away so that most of her porch remained in darkness. I dug around under the big pot of ivy next to the front door for Lula Mae's spare key. As I suspected, it wasn't there.

A shiver charged up my spine. Maybe searching for Percy alone, at night, wasn't such a brilliant idea, after all.

The voice inside my head told me not to be such a chicken. Percy was probably long gone by now. Possibly halfway across the country. And if he was still hanging around . . . it's not like he'd murdered Camilla. All his conquests seem to agree that he was a con man and a thief, but not a killer.

Mustering my courage, I pulled open the screen door and undid the lock. It was probably nothing more than my imagination, but I couldn't shake the feeling something horrible waited for me inside.

Before I could talk myself out of it, I pushed into the house. Right off, I was struck by how cold and empty the place seemed. It made me long for the warm, cozy feeling that always greeted me whenever I usually came to visit.

From somewhere near the kitchen there came a scuffling sound. My heart nearly leaped out of my chest. I froze in place, waiting for it to be repeated. But all was silent. Probably just a mouse, I concluded.

Which might explain the smell.

Bypassing the light switch, I flipped on my flashlight and moved further into the room. "Percy, it's me, Kate," I called softly, "Lula Mae's niece. Are you in here?"

There was no welcoming, "Hi, there. So glad to see you."

Moving the feeble beam of light slowly around the room, I passed over, then came back to a brown lump lying between the coffee table and the couch. A lump that had no business being there. A lump that I soon realized had arms and legs attached.

My heart started beating so fast, I was afraid I was seconds away from complete cardiac arrest. Repelled, yet drawn, to the object sprawled on the floor, I inched forward. And found myself staring into the deadest pair of blue eyes I'd ever seen.

Suddenly, my knees threatened to buckle. I groped for the nearest chair and collapsed in a heap, struggling to breathe.

Then it hit me: Maybe I wasn't alone with that—thing on the floor. Maybe whoever had done this horrible deed was still in the house. A surge of adrenaline slammed through my body that was more powerful than any street drug. I pushed to my feet and was out the door in a flash. And barreled down the front steps, right into the arms of Lieutenant Griggs.

"What's going on here?" he barked. "We just received a call about a possible break-in."

My teeth began to chatter so hard, I had trouble answering. "It's Percy," I finally managed to say. "Inside. I think . . . I think he's dead."

Steven handed me over to another officer and pulled out his weapon. He wasn't gone long. When he returned, things really started to hum. Other police units arrived, followed by a crime scene van, then a swarm of curious neighbors.

By the time Steven got back to me, his manner had grown stiff and formal. "I need to know what you were doing here tonight."

Lifting my chin, I said, "I came by to pick up a few things Lula Mae needed."

"Funny. I don't see your truck parked outside. Did you walk over here? It must be a good ten miles from your mother's place. And what about the lights? Were you stumbling around in the dark because you wanted to conserve energy?"

I folded my arms across my chest and tried not to look intimidated. "Shouldn't you be concentrating on finding out who murdered Percy? Not standing here, harassing an innocent, law-abiding citizen."

His brows arched. "Who said anything about murder?"

"It's perfectly obvious. I mean . . ."

He began to bombard me with questions. "Did you touch the body? Hear, or see anything suspicious?"

Realizing I had no choice, I told him all I knew. Which wasn't much. When I finished, he said something about not leaving town, then sent Joe to escort me back to my truck.

As we plodded down the sidewalk, I tried to engage the young cop in conversation. "Think Percy died from a blow to the head like Camilla?"

His brown eyes cut toward me. "No comment," he said, keeping his voice neutral.

Who did he think he was talking to—the press?

I tried again. "I'm no expert, but it looked like he might've been there a while."

Again, no response on his part.

I tried several more times, but nothing I said could get the young cop to budge from his "no comment" stance. When we reached our destination, he tossed out a, "Have a nice day, ma'am," and scurried away as if the hounds from hell were after him.

I scrambled inside my truck and sat there a few minutes, enjoying the quiet before the storm. Then I plucked up my courage and went home to break the news to Happy and Lula Mae.

They weren't easy to rouse from bed. Each struggled into almost identical housecoats, flowered tents with snaps down the front, and followed me downstairs. They slumped down at the kitchen table, while I put on a pot of coffee. As they struggled to keep their eyes open, I rummaged around until I found Happy's stash of chocolate chip cookies and arranged them carefully on a white china plate. When I couldn't think of anything else to do, I joined them at the table.

"I'd like to know what's so all-fired important that you have to drag us out of bed in the middle of the night," Happy said.

"Yeah, I'd like to know the answer to that question myself," Lula Mae said. "You do realize that you've interrupted my beauty sleep. If I don't get at least eight hours of sleep, I'll look like a raccoon in the morning."

Apparently, her beauty problems didn't extend to her waistline, because she grabbed two cookies off the plate and started munching. I got up, poured three coffees, then sat back down. For once, the aroma of chocolate failed to spark my appetite. "I guess you're both wondering why I dragged you out of bed."

"Isn't that what I just asked you?" Happy said. The coffee

seemed to have done its job. Her eyes were fully open, and brimming with suspicion.

I fidgeted in my seat, not sure how to begin. "I thought it would be easier if you heard it from me," I finally said. "The police found Percy."

"Thank goodness." Lula Mae instantly brightened. "Maybe we can finally get some answers. Did he say who—"

"What do you mean by 'found'?" Happy zoomed in on my choice of words. "Are you trying to tell us something has happened to Percy?"

I sighed. "There's no easy way to say this." I avoided eye contact with Lula Mae. "The police found his body a couple of hours ago. He was at Lula Mae's house. In the middle of her living room."

"That's impossible." Lula Mae gripped the edge of the table. "Percy couldn't be . . . not in my . . ." Using the table for support, she hoisted herself up, then stumbled out of the kitchen.

I assumed Happy would go after her. But she had other things on her mind. "I'd like to know what Percy was doing at Lula Mae's house. And, for that matter, what were you doing there?"

I belted out the excuse I'd concocted on the drive home. "I was doing Lula Mae a favor, checking out her place, making sure everything was locked up tight."

Ignoring my explanation, Happy stormed on. "We're supposed to be a team. We're supposed to share information. And here you go trotting off on your own again, without so much as a word to the rest of us. What were you thinking?"

"I didn't mean to—"

"I don't want to hear it." She shot up from her chair. "You could've been killed tonight. Or been lying in a ditch somewhere while we were sound asleep in our beds." Giving me the "you ungrateful child" look, she bolted from the room.

"I was never in any real danger," I called after her.

CHAPTER THIRTY-THREE

Tuesday morning, Steven showed up bright and early on our doorstep. "What do you want?" I asked, reluctant to unlatch the screen door to let him in.

"Sorry, Kate, but I'm here to take Lula Mae in for questioning."

My stomach twisted into knots. "You have no right to haul her down to headquarters. She hasn't done anything."

"Don't make this any harder than it has to be."

"There are plenty of other people you could be talking to. How about Tony, or Keith Davenport? Either one of them could've found out that Percy killed Camilla and—"

He shook his head wearily. "I don't have a choice about this."

"Of course you do." I couldn't just stand there and let him haul Lula Mae off without a fight. She was much too fragile. "What about Percy's notebook? Any one of those women he conned money out of could've killed him."

"Lula Mae's name was in that notebook," he reminded me.

I crossed my arms and glared at him. "You think a woman who relocates spiders from her house to the backyard is a killer?"

"He was found in her house," he laid out his logic. "The doors weren't forced, no windows broken."

I unlatched the screen door and stepped outside. "Because someone took the key from under the pot of ivy on her front porch and let themselves in."

"Who?"

My eyes narrowed. "Isn't that what you're paid to find out?"

He sighed. "Look, I have a hard time believing Lula Mae would kill anybody, too. But all the evidence points to her."

"You're telling me Lula Mae lured Percy to her house, killed him in cold blood, then rushed back to our house and fell peacefully asleep in her bed. Because that's where she was when I got home. Sound asleep. In the guest-room bed."

"The evidence says—"

I cut him off. "I don't care what the evidence says. I know in my gut that Lula Mae doesn't have what it takes to murder anybody."

He stared at me through bloodshot eyes. "I've already taken a lot of heat for not arresting her for Camilla's murder. Now, with a second murder, I can't continue to ignore the facts."

"What facts?"

He ticked off the points on his fingers. "Number one: The man was killed in her house. Number two: She recently learned about all the other women in her fiancé's life. Number three: The man stole some of your uncle's belongings. And, number four: The murder weapon belongs to her."

Alarm bells started clanging in my head. "What murder weapon?"

"A Colt .22."

My knees wanted to buckle. "There was a lot of blood, but I just assumed he was killed the same way as Camilla."

"It was pretty dark in there," he said. "And you were in pretty bad shape when we found you."

Sanity began to return. "But don't you see, that eliminates Lula Mae from your pool of suspects. I know for a fact, she doesn't own a gun. Or know how to use one, for that matter."

"Just like she didn't know how to drive a car."

"That was different."

"Look," he went on more gently, "the weapon was found in

190

Lula Mae's kitchen."

"Then the killer must have left it there hoping to frame Lula Mae. Besides, I'm positive she doesn't own a gun."

"Maybe not," he said, then nailed the lid on soundly, "but your uncle did."

"Even if he did," I said, trying to come up with a reasonable explanation, "half the town knows where Lula Mae keeps her spare key. They could've easily plundered through her house and found Uncle George's gun."

"She purchased a box of ammo a few days ago."

I opened my mouth, but couldn't think of any rebuttal, and snapped it shut.

"Believe me—" he began.

I held up a hand. "I don't want to hear it. If it's the last thing I do, I will find out who killed Percy. And when I do, don't even think about trying to worm your way back into my life. Because we're finished. Do you hear me? Finished."

Before Steven could get Lula Mae into the squad car, he had to go through the whole process again with Happy, whose claws were razor sharp. "When I get through with you, young man, you'll be praying to even get work as a garbage man in this town."

He sighed. "If there's anyone in this town capable of accomplishing that feat, it would be you, Mrs. Spencer."

As they led a dazed and confused Lula Mae out the door, she kept repeating, "But I didn't do anything." Thankfully, Steven was gentle with her; otherwise, Happy might have ripped him to shreds right on the spot.

"Don't you worry, hon," Happy said as the officer helped Lula Mae into the car. "I'm going inside right now and put in a call to Sam Hazelberry, so don't you go answering any of their questions until he gets there. Do you hear me? Not one single one."

Lula Mae nodded and repeated, "But I didn't do anything."

"That's right, hon." Happy's words were directed to Lula Mae, but her gaze was glued to Steven. "You just keep right on telling them that. Sooner or later, they'll start listening."

While Happy continued to console Lula Mae, Steven drew me aside. "I'm really sorry about this, Kate. If there was any way—"

Tears clouded my eyes. "I'm never going to forget this."

His face was etched in sadness. "I know."

Turning away, he walked slowly back to his squad car. Happy and I stood there like a pair of sentinels until his car disappeared from sight, then we went inside and Happy put in a call to Sam Hazelberry. "Sam, I know you're there. Turn off that blasted machine and pick up the phone. I need your help."

Apparently, Sam had the good sense to be in his office and picked up the phone. While she filled him in on the details of his new case, I went into the other room, got out paper and pen, and began to jot down the names of every person I could think of who might have a reason for killing Percy.

The first on the list was Stella Barnes, who'd admitted giving Percy money to purchase bakery equipment. And since she also considered herself the man's fiancée, I put a star beside her name. Learning she wasn't the only woman engaged to the man had to be painful. But was it enough to drive her to murder?

The next name I listed was Lucille Crandell. She seemed fairly open about her feelings for Percy—all of them negative. But someone had been hiding out at her house.

Fran Parker's name came next. She didn't strike me as belonging in the same category as the other two, but I couldn't rule her out. Despite what she'd told us, the notebook tucked away in Percy's closet indicated that he'd conned her out of a great deal of money. At least, that was his plan. Whether he succeeded or not was something we'd have to find out.

All three women might consider Camilla a rival for Percy's affections, thus tying them to her murder. Add Lula Mae's relationship with Percy to the mixture, and it might've been the spark needed to push the killer into framing Lula Mae for both murders.

And what about Mrs. Mayfield? She gave Percy money for an oven. I couldn't rule her out. No matter how much I liked her.

As for Camilla's murder, Tony was definitely in the running for that deed. His business was in serious trouble. To the tune of how much, I didn't know. But considering how secretive he'd been about his financial situation, I'd say he was on the verge of bankruptcy.

Underneath Tony's name, I scribbled Keith's. He was facing a messy and costly divorce. Of course, lots of men get divorced without resorting to murder, but you could never tell. Besides, his sneaking around out by the lake didn't sit well with me.

Next, I wrote down Evelyn Davenport's name. Under motive, I listed the same explanation as I had written beside Tony's name—a desperate need for money.

As far as I was concerned, each of the Davenports had a good reason to kill Percy. The possibility that he'd murdered Camilla may have pushed one of them over the edge. And even if he hadn't killed her, the mere fact that he was planning to con her out of a sizable chunk of money was motive enough for murder in my book.

While I was reflecting on the implications of that idea, Happy dashed into the room. "Now that I have that situation under control, it's time to find out who murdered Percy so we can get Lula Mae out of that horrid place."

I eased the paper I was working on into the desk drawer. "It may not be that easy."

"Nonsense. We know Lula Mae didn't kill anybody, so we'll

just go down that list you made until we find the scumbag who did."

"What makes you so sure I made a list?"

Happy rolled her eyes heavenward.

"Okay." I gave in. "So I did make a list, but that doesn't mean we can go running around town accusing people of murder." It occurred to me that I was beginning to sound a lot like Steven. "We could be putting ourselves in a lot of danger."

"Young lady, the only danger you're going to be in is getting your skull cracked open if you don't grab that list and get moving. I do not intend to sit around here twiddling my thumbs while the police harass my baby sister."

"Well . . ." I hesitated. "I suppose there's no harm in asking a few questions."

CHAPTER THIRTY-FOUR

By the time we reached Lucille's old Victorian, the place was sealed up tighter than a vault. The curtains were closed and none of the usual sounds of occupancy could be heard from the front porch.

Happy's knocking soon turned to pounding. "Lucille, I know you're in there. Open this door, right now."

"It's no use," I said. "She's not home."

"She's in there all right," Happy said with conviction. "I saw a curtain move."

"It was probably just your imagination."

"I know what I saw." Bolting off the front porch, she marched over to the garage and tried to peek through the narrow band of windows that ran along the front. I say "tried," because she was too short to actually see inside.

"Don't just stand there like an idiot," she yelled. "Come over here and see if her car's parked inside."

The car was in there all right, but I wasn't about to tell Happy. No telling what she might do. "Not there," I said. "Guess we'd better head over to Fran's house and come back later."

Happy wasn't pleased by the idea. But since there was little she could do short of breaking in, she settled for giving the garage door a good, solid kick, then followed me back to the truck.

Ten minutes later we arrived at Fran's to confront the same

situation—a closed-up house and no answer to our knock.

"If you're looking for Fran," a deep, male voice said, "she's not home."

Startled, we spun around to face the best-looking hunk I'd seen in ages. Make that ever. He was tall, at least six-four. Had long brown hair and a beautiful set of white teeth. "You are looking for Fran, aren't you?" he asked.

My eyes locked onto the muscles in his arms, which strained to break free from the flimsy, cotton T-shirt he had on. "Uh, yeah. We're looking for Fran," I said, and realized I sounded like a complete idiot.

He dazzled us with a smile. "You just missed her."

As I gazed into his clear blue eyes, my breath seemed to hang up in my throat. "Do you live around here?" I finally managed to ask, my voice coming out kind of raspy.

He pointed toward a rambling white house. "Next door."

Happy eyed him suspiciously. "That's old man Sweeney's place."

"I know." He laughed. "He's my grandfather. You may have heard that he hasn't been doing all that well these last few months. I decided to come down and help out for a while." He stuck out his hand. "Where are my manners? I'm Thomas Sweeney, Charles's boy."

He was no boy, I thought, taking his hand. Anybody with eyes could see that. "I'm Kate, and this is my mother . . ." I rattled around in my brain for the name. "Happy Spencer."

For once Happy seemed to be at a loss for words. Thomas held out his hand, but she shrank back as if he'd held out a red-hot poker. He shrugged, let his hand drop to his side.

"How's Mr. Sweeney doing?" I asked, diverting his attention from my mother's lack of manners.

He turned back to me. "He's doing great. Especially since I've been mixing him up some of my energy shakes."

I wasn't sure I wanted to know the answer, but asked anyway, "What's in them?"

"I start off with a base of wheat-grass juice, add a touch of brewer's yeast, throw in various vegetables, depending on what I have on hand, and presto—instant energy. Would you like to try one?"

A tight knot of revulsion formed in my stomach. "No, thanks."

"How about you, Mrs. Spencer, you want one?"

"I have more energy than I know what to do with, young man."

"Well, if you change your mind, the offer is always open."

Back to her normal self, Happy said, "Young man, do you have any idea when Fran will be back in town?"

"That's hard to say, ma'am. But I think she plans on being gone for quite some time."

"Why is that?" she asked.

"Because I just helped her load about forty million pieces of luggage into that car of hers."

"I don't suppose she happened to mention where she was headed," I said.

His brow puckered in thought. "South America. Brazil maybe."

"No extradition policy," Happy whispered to me.

Thomas walked us back to the truck and helped Happy inside. "Do you happen to recall if Fran was home last Wednesday night?" she asked him.

"The night that woman got murdered?" He shook his head. "I didn't see her until the next morning. I was taking Granddad to the eye doctor and saw her pull in."

After getting Happy settled, Thomas came around and opened my door. Normally, I prided myself on being an independent woman, but just this once, I relented and accepted his help.

As we pulled away, I took a last glimpse at our Adonis, gave the horn a tap, then stuck my hand out the window and gave a wave. Thomas returned my wave before walking back to his grandfather's place.

Happy snorted.

I met her accusing stare. "What?"

"I thought you were sweet on that policeman of yours."

"That was before he arrested Lula Mae. Now he's on my list of highly disreputable people."

"Good." Happy sounded pleased.

Ignoring the nagging sense of lost that assailed me, I stepped on the gas.

Though I was driving well over the posted speed limit, apparently, it wasn't fast enough for Happy. "Can't you go any faster? The way you're poking around, we'll never get through all those names on your list."

CHAPTER THIRTY-FIVE

As I stepped on the gas, Happy's brow puckered in thought. "You do realize that our killer might have just flown the country."

The same thought had been running through my mind. "Hold on. We don't know that Fran killed anybody. The way Thomas talked, she didn't get home until after Camilla was killed, and she might have an alibi for Percy's murder."

"Innocent people don't run from the law."

"We have no proof Fran is running from the law. She may have had this trip planned for months."

Happy eyes narrowed. "Are you defending her?"

"No, but I'm not ready to condemn her just because she happens to enjoy traveling. If I had her money, I'd probably be jet-setting around the world, too."

"Face it, young lady, if you had a man living next door to you who looked like the specimen we just encountered, would you feel the need to go gallivanting around the globe to meet men?"

She had me there. "I guess not."

"I didn't think so." She tapped her foot against the floorboard. "Didn't Thomas say he just helped her load her luggage? If we hurry, maybe we can catch her before her flight leaves."

I sped up.

For once, luck was with us. We spotted Fran's car at a gas station near the on ramp to the interstate and swerved in behind her. Before I had time to slam the truck into park, Happy had already scrambled out of the cab. I bolted after her.

"Fran Parker." Happy smiled, as if she hadn't seen her old friend in ages. "Fancy meeting you here. We were just by your place a few minutes ago."

Fran seemed overwhelmed by Happy's exuberant greeting. She removed the hose from her gas tank and returned it to the pump. "Look, I'm kind of in a hurry." She tore off her credit card receipt. "If you don't mind, maybe we can talk later."

"How much later?" Happy asked. "Say, ten or twenty years from now?"

Fran gave Happy a puzzled look. "What's the matter with you? Are you on drugs, or did somebody fry your brain?"

Time to reel in our suspect. "Why don't you tell us about the money you gave Percy," I suggested.

Both women turned to stare at me with their mouths hanging open. "What money?" Happy sent me an accusing glare.

"According to the notebook I found in Percy's closet, I'd say around ten grand."

I saw the fury in Happy's face and knew I'd pay for not telling her about the notebook. But I didn't have time to worry about it now. Not with a murder charge hanging over Lula Mae's head. "How much?" I asked.

"That little weasel." Fran kicked her back tire. "I should've known he'd keep a record of his dirty little business. I guess that's why the police were sniffing around the other day, asking questions about how I met Percy, and wanting to know if I'd given him any money."

"Why didn't you tell us about the money the day we stopped by?" Happy demanded, taking charge of the situation.

"I guess I should have, but I was too embarrassed. Imagine me, a woman of the world, getting taken in by a con man. I thought that if I pretended it never happened, it would all go away. Nobody would have to know how foolish I'd been. But I should've known better. Once a man like Percy gets hold of you, it's hard to shake him loose."

"Unless he's eliminated from the picture," I said.

She gave me a funny look, like I was the crazy one. "Did your brain get fried, too? You sound like one of those Mafia characters in the movies."

I glanced at Happy. "Maybe she didn't hear the news."

Fran's gaze shifted from me to Happy. "What news?"

"Percy's dead," Happy said. "Murdered, from the looks of it."

Fran's eyes widened. "What's going on in this town? First Camilla goes and gets herself killed, now Percy?"

"Were you in town the night Camilla was murdered?" I asked.

Fran's eyes narrowed. "Why would you ask me that?"

I did some fast thinking. "I was just wondering who told you she'd been murdered. It didn't seem like you'd been home long enough for the grapevine to reach you."

Fran seemed to relax. "Truth is: Pricilla told me."

Happy looked as shocked as I felt. "Pricilla?" I tried to wrap my mind around the idea. "The woman who works . . . worked for Camilla?"

"Why on earth would she call you?" Happy demanded. "It's not like you run in the same circles."

"Because, with Camilla dead, she needed a job."

"But the family—" I began.

"Will probably sell the place. And, besides, who wants to work in a house where someone was murdered."

"What about Saturday night?" I asked. "Did you have a date, or spend the evening with friends?"

Her eyes settled on me. "Was that when Percy was killed?"

I didn't comment.

She drew herself up stiffly. "Well, you can eliminate me as a suspect. I was having dinner with my next door neighbor,

Thomas Sweeney, and his grandson, Tommy. After dinner, we watched a couple of old movies. I didn't get home until well after midnight."

I wasn't sure what time Percy had met his end, but Fran seemed open enough about her whereabouts. And, though she had good reason to want Percy dead, I couldn't think of a reasonable motive for Camilla's murder. The only thing that came to mind was Camilla's attempt to keep Fran out of the country club. But that hardly seemed worth going to prison over. My gut said she didn't do it.

Happy must have come to the same conclusion. Glancing at her watch, she said, "Well, I guess we'd better be on our way. Give me a call when you get back. We'll have lunch."

Fran stood there shaking her head in bewilderment as we scrambled back into the truck. I didn't blame her. I felt pretty bewildered myself.

For the next few minutes Happy and I drove aimlessly around town, trying to agree on our next move. Finally, I succumbed to her suggestion and headed back to Lucille's place.

As I expected, the house was still closed up tight. But I knew there was no stopping her this time. One way or another, she'd get inside. Even if she had to break down the front door to do it. Which seemed like a distinct possibility at the moment.

"Lucille Crandell," Happy yelled as she pounded on the door, "I know you're in there. And I don't intend to leave peacefully this time. If I have to, I'll bust out a window. So you might as well get your butt over here and open this door."

Lucille must have realized Happy meant business because the next thing I knew, the door flew open. As she hustled us inside, I noticed her creamy-white skin was all splotched, as if she'd been crying. And her coal black hair looked as if it hadn't seen a brush in days.

Happy got right up in Lucille's face. Well, as close as a woman

Happy's size could get in somebody's face. "Why didn't you open the door the first time we came by?"

Lucille took a step back. "Because I knew you wanted to talk about Percy." Her voice sounded all quivery. "And I never want to hear that man's name again."

Happy's brows knotted. "Why is that?"

"You know very well why. Everybody in town is talking about what a fool I've been. I'm so ashamed. I haven't been out of the house in two days. Not even to go to the grocery store. The fact is I'll probably never be able to hold my head up in this town again. I'll have to move somewhere far away—like Alaska, where nobody's ever heard of me."

Happy didn't seem to know how to react to this impassioned revelation. "You've heard that Percy was murdered, haven't you?"

What little color there was in Lucille's face faded. "You must be mistaken. When he didn't come back, I just figured he'd skipped town. I had no idea . . . I just can't believe . . ."

Oblivious to Lucille's distress, Happy rattled on. "Now, Lucille, we need your help. The police seem to think Lula Mae killed Percy. But you and I both know . . ." Her voice trailed off as Lucille crumpled to the floor.

By the time we'd revived her and explained what'd happened, a good half hour had passed. "I can't believe Percy's gone." A fresh trail of tears spilled down Lucille's cheeks. "He had his faults, certainly, but he had a way of making a woman feel special. Like you really mattered to someone."

I shook my head. I'd never understand this hold Percy seemed to have over women. Maybe it had something to do with that old saying, "Love is blind." Or my personal theory, "Love sucks the brains out of normally reasonable, sane women."

Not ready to let her off the hook, I said, "What can you tell us about this business Camilla and Percy were planning on starting?"

It took a moment for the words to register. "Percy was never going into business with Camilla."

"Come on," I said, "we all know he hit her up for money to open a bakery."

"He wanted money all right, but not to open a bakery. He had his eye on a piece of property along the waterfront. He wanted to open some upscale restaurant. You know, one of those places where they serve those overpriced meals that leave you feeling hungry when you're done eating."

Happy snorted. "If the man put half as much energy into work instead of conning women out of money, he'd be a millionaire by now."

Lucille sighed. "Look, I know you don't like Percy, not after what he did to Lula Mae, but the man's not a killer. Whoever murdered Camilla must've thought he knew something, and killed him to keep him from going to the cops."

Time to shake her up a little. "Tell us about the money he conned you out of," I said.

"Like I told you," she said, beginning to sound agitated, "I didn't give him any money. Remember"—she looked to Happy for support—"how he dumped me when I wouldn't sell any of my antiques?"

"I remember," Happy agreed.

That may be. But her reaction to Percy's death seemed way out of proportion for someone who'd only dated the man for a short period of time. "Percy kept detailed records," I said, and watched her face for a reaction.

If possible, she grew even paler. "But I didn't give him any money. Well," she amended, "hardly any money."

Happy looked to me. "According to his notebook, only a few hundred."

"Hardly worth killing a man over," she said.

"What about that shaving kit in your bathroom?" I said. "And don't give us that line about it belonging to your nephew."

Lucille seemed to shrink before our very eyes. "I didn't mean to deceive you." She shot an apologetic look in Happy's direction. "But Percy knew the police would focus on him and never look for the real killer, so I let him hide out here for a few days. Only until he could figure out what to do about his situation."

"How noble of him to leave Lula Mae to take the fall," I said, my voice full of sarcasm.

She glared at me. "What kind of person do you think I am? Lula Mae is my friend. I care about her as much as you do."

"You have a strange way of showing it," I said. Then I regretted it when the tears started up again and we had to waste another half hour calming her down.

"We really should be going," I said finally. "We have other stops to make."

I could tell Happy was torn between consoling an old friend and finding a killer. I gave her a nudge, then nodded toward the door.

"Don't worry, hon." Happy got to her feet. "We'll be back soon to check on you."

The moment we cleared the door, Happy said, "Why did you drag me out of there so fast? I'm not sure Lucille ought to be alone right now."

"Have you forgotten about Lula Mae?"

"Of course I haven't forgotten about her."

"Good," I said. "Because she's family. And she needs our help more than Lucille does."

Chapter Thirty-Six

When we arrived at Stella's, Happy seemed reluctant to get out of the truck. "Something wrong?" I asked. "You haven't been this quiet since the time you backed into old man McCarthy's car."

"I'm fine," Happy snapped.

"There's really no need for you to go inside. I can—"

She climbed out of the truck. "It's my sister's life that's on the line here."

Though she sounded as feisty as ever, I noticed her usual pep was missing as we made our way to the door. She even sagged against the door frame, leaving me to ring the bell.

Stella answered, wearing the same pink quilted housecoat she'd worn during our last visit. Her nose was red, and her eyes puffy. "Oh, Happy. I just heard the news about Percy on the radio. I'm sure Lula Mae must be devastated."

"She is," Happy said. "Especially since the police have arrested her for his murder."

Stella's eyes popped open in disbelief. "That's crazy. Lula Mae's no killer."

"Unfortunately," I said, "the police in this town have little experience in these matters. Offhand, I could name at least four people who had good reason to kill Percy."

Stella's gaze shifted from me to Happy. "Is that why you're here? Because you think I had something to do with his murder?"

I could sense Happy's unease. Stella was an old childhood friend, but Lula Mae was family. And with Happy, family comes first. "Of course not," Happy said.

Her answer had been too long in coming. "I can't believe it." Stella's voice rose by several decibels. "You actually think I had something to do with his murder."

"I don't think anything of the kind." Happy hurried to repair the damage she'd done to their friendship. "I just thought you might have some idea about who might've wanted to harm him."

Stella eyes narrowed. "And how would I know that?"

Happy swept past her friend and snagged a spot on the sofa. "Oh, for goodness sakes, you were engaged to the man. You must know something about who his enemies were."

"Lula Mae was engaged to Percy, too," Stella pointed out, "but I don't see you badgering her."

Happy struggled to hold on to her patience. "Like I told you, she's being questioned by the police."

"No," Stella corrected. "You said the police arrested her. Which is it?"

Happy pursed her lips in annoyance. "The police took her in for questioning, but they'll never let her go. All the evidence seems to point to her."

Stella sagged down in the nearest chair. "I can't believe this is happening. We've always had such a nice, safe town. Now people are being murdered left and right, and innocent people are going to jail."

"Everything seems centered around Percy," I said. "He has a history of cheating . . ." I started to say gullible, but changed it to ". . . innocent women out of their life's savings. Maybe one of them decided to get even. Or one of the women's relatives discovered their inheritance was being siphoned off and decided to put a stop to it."

"Maybe," Stella said. "But Percy wasn't like that with me. He was the sweetest, most adorable man on earth. If you knew how alive he made me feel when I was with him . . ." Her face softened. "He opened up a whole new world of possibilities for me."

"All that sweetness was just a ploy," I said, taking a seat beside Happy. "The man was just after your money."

The soft glow faded. She sprang to her feet and began to pace the room. "Why should I believe anything you say? The last time you were here you made up that ridiculous story about Percy being engaged to Lula Mae."

I felt the vein in my temple begin to throb. "It wasn't a story."

"Of course it was. In fact, it had to be an out-and-out lie, because Percy told me—" She broke off, realizing her mistake.

Happy jumped on this nugget of information. "How could he have told you anything? The man's been hiding out since the night Camilla was murdered."

"I spoke to him long before any of that happened," Stella quickly said.

"That's a lie," I said. "You didn't even know Lula Mae was engaged until we told you. And that happened after Camilla's murder. Time to fess up. When did you see him last?" I scooted forward in my seat. "Yesterday? The day before?"

Stella dropped into the chair across from me and covered her face with her hands. After several minutes of Happy's none-too-gentle prodding, she finally admitted, "I saw him a couple of days ago."

"But Percy was killed a couple of days ago," Happy said. "You might've been one of the last people to see him." A speculative gleam dawned in her eyes. "Unless you—"

Stella was back on her feet. "I didn't kill him, if that's what you're thinking. Percy was very much alive when I left him."

"What time was that?" Happy asked.

Stella shoulders sagged. "It must've been around two o'clock Saturday afternoon," she said. Then added more softly, "We met at Lula Mae's house."

Eyes blazing, Happy flew off the couch. "You knew Percy was hiding out in Lula Mae's house and you didn't call the police."

Stella shrank back. "What was I supposed to do? The man needed help. And he had no one else to turn to."

Knowing Percy, I asked the obvious question. "How much money did you give him?"

Her face turned a delicate shade of pink. "About four hundred dollars," she said, staring down at her feet. "It was all I could come up with on such short notice."

"You know you're going to have to tell the police about all this," I said.

Her head shot up. "I can't do that. They might think I had something to do with his murder."

Words flew out of Happy's mouth that soon had Stella weeping. Before we left, Happy wrangled a promise out of Stella to head straight to police headquarters and tell Lieutenant Griggs everything she knew.

"What do you think?" I asked as we climbed into the truck. "Is she telling the truth?"

"About the money, or about killing Percy?"

"Both."

She thought about it a minute. "I think she'd tell us whatever we wanted to hear. As long as it covered her butt."

So much for the friendship they'd shared over the years.

Under normal circumstances, Happy would be spending quality time with me on our drive over to the Davenports'. Translation: she'd be dishing out the latest gossip she'd accumulated during the past week. But the circumstances weren't normal, and Happy sat stiffly beside me, her eyes focused on the road, strangely silent.

"Are you all right?"

"I'm fine." Her voice came out flat, dull, without any of her usual pep.

My worry muscles shifted into high gear. I stole a look at her face. Did her skin look more saggy than usual? I couldn't be sure. But there was no mistaking the dark circles under her eyes. She had the bruised look of someone battling a long-term illness.

"Maybe we ought to swing by Bessie's for a roast beef sandwich," I suggested.

Happy shot that idea down fast. "Lula Mae's in deep trouble. Now is the time for action, not for stuffing our faces."

Five minutes later, we pulled into Camilla's driveway. Henry, the faithful gardener, was perched atop the riding mower, moving methodically back and forth across the lawn. He waved as we headed up the walk, and yelled something we couldn't make out over the roar of the engine.

I rang the bell and waited for someone to come to the door. Tony Davenport answered, looking almost as bad as Happy. He had lost weight. Ten pounds, at least. And there was a pasty tint to his skin that reminded me of one of those vampire shows.

"What do you want?" He glared at me like I had the plague.

"Don't take that tone of voice with my daughter, young man," Happy said. "I know your mama raised you better than that."

Bright dots of pink suffused his cheeks as his attention shifted to the pint-sized woman beside me. "Yes, ma'am, she did." He stepped back. "Won't you please come in," he said politely.

Back in control, Happy sashayed past him, leaving me to follow in her wake. Bypassing the room where Camilla had met her end, Happy marched straight to the sunroom. After settling into one of the brightly cushioned chairs, she got down to business. "We've come to find out what you know about Percy

Moss's death."

A shadow slid across his face. "What did you say?"

Happy wiggled forward in her seat. "Here I thought only old people were deaf." She flicked an impatient hand in the air. As if speaking to someone from another country, she slowly repeated, "We've come to find out what you know about Percy Moss's death."

Sparks of anger flashed in his eyes. "I understand English, Mrs. Spencer. What I don't understand is why you're asking me that question."

Happy's backbone stiffened. "Are you trying to rile me, young man?"

"No, ma'am, I'm not. I just don't understand why you think I know anything about his death. I've never even met the man."

"I'm asking," Happy said, barely holding on to her temper, "because your mother was right sweet on the man, if I recall."

"So were lots of other women around town," he countered, "including your sister."

That did it! Happy geared up for an all-out assault. "How dare you accuse—"

"I'm not accusing anybody," he broke in. "I'm simply pointing out that several people in this town had good reason to want the man dead. Your sister included."

I'd kept silent long enough. "Where were you Saturday night?"

His ice-blue eyes fastened on me. "I could ask you the same question. You had as much reason to hate the guy as anyone else."

I felt as if I'd slammed into a brick wall. I'd never thought of myself as a suspect. And I didn't much like the idea. "I, uh . . ."

"It's not so funny when the shoe is on the other foot, is it?"

Before I spit out a reply, Evelyn Davenport strode into the room carrying a steaming cup of coffee. Her hair and makeup were perfectly done, yet she had on a chartreuse silk robe as if she had just stepped out of bed. "Well, if it isn't the detective duo," she said. "Are you here to round up suspects in the gigolo murder?"

Murder was on my mind, all right. Evelyn Davenport's.

"Don't get sassy with me, young lady." There was an indignant tone to Happy's voice that promised trouble.

Evelyn flopped down in the chair beside Happy. "What would you call a man who made his living fleecing innocent women out of their life savings?"

Happy ignored the question. "Your husband was just telling us that he has no alibi for Saturday night. How about you? Do you have an alibi? Because the way I see it, you have as much reason to hate Percy as anybody else."

Tony started to speak, but Evelyn cut him off. "Of course, he has an alibi for Saturday night. He was here with me, celebrating our anniversary."

A flicker of surprise slid across Tony's face. "She's right," he said quickly. "We were here celebrating our anniversary. Together. All night."

Did they think we were a couple of backwoods hicks?

Happy gave a loud snort to show what she thought of their alibi.

"Besides," Evelyn went on, "even if we did want to go out, there's not much nightlife around this place. Most of the town shuts down before midnight."

She had a point. This was a small town. Not many places stayed open late. "I'm surprised you didn't drive into Mobile for dinner, or head over to New Orleans."

"Under the circumstances, that would've been totally inappropriate," Tony said.

Happy was ready to burst at the seams. "What about that cook of Camilla's? Did she fix you two some fancy dinner for your anniversary?"

"Not that it's any of your business," Evelyn said, "but we've given Pricilla some time off. I cooked our dinner."

They were in Happy's territory now. "What was on the menu?" She snickered. "Chicken noodle soup, fresh from the can?"

Evelyn's eyes became slits of fire. "This conversation is over." She got to her feet. "Tony, please show these ladies, and I use the term loosely, to the door."

"You'd better hope the police don't show up on your doorstep before you come up with a more convincing story," I called over my shoulder as Tony ushered us from the room. "Or they'll be arresting you for Percy's murder."

"The way I hear it, the police already have a suspect in custody," Evelyn yelled back.

Happy whirled around and started back in Evelyn's direction. Afraid her fury might get her thrown into the cell next to Lula Mae, I grabbed her arm and dragged her down the hall to the front door.

"It might be better if you two don't come back," Tony said as he herded us through the door.

"Wait a minute." I spun around. "What about Keith? Where was he—"

Before I could finish my sentence, he slammed the door in our faces.

CHAPTER THIRTY-SEVEN

Sam Hazelton, occupying the swing on our front porch, watched as we pulled into the driveway. Tall and thin, he still sported a full head of hair, even though it was solid white now, instead of the dark brown it had once been.

Happy bolted from the truck and practically flew up the front steps. "How's Lula Mae holding up? Is she inside? I know the poor thing must be frightened. I'd better go inside and—" She started toward the door.

"Lula Mae isn't inside." Sam stood up, towering over both of us.

Happy's eyes narrowed. "Why not?"

Sam regarded her for a moment with clear, gray eyes. "She's not inside because Lieutenant Griggs has her locked up downtown."

Happy's face contorted in fury. If Steven J. Griggs had been in the room with us, I think she would've plucked his heart out with her bare hands. "Why, I ought to—"

"You should have told me the murder victim was Lula Mae's fiancé."

"Ex-fiancé." Happy averted her gaze. "And I didn't see why that was important."

"Come on. You've watched enough cop shows to know the first place the police look in a murder investigation is at the people who are close to the victim. And I'd say, being a man's fiancée, puts Lula Mae right at the top of the list. Especially since it appears he has been"—he cleared his throat—"less than faithful in his affections. Added to that, Lula Mae's fingerprints are all over the murder weapon."

"That's the part I don't understand," I said. "Lula Mae hates guns."

He looked at me. "She claims that it's your fault her prints are on the gun."

I didn't have to feign surprise. "My fault? I don't see how that's possible."

"She said you got her so spooked over Camilla's death that she had Happy drive her to the store to buy a box of bullets, then over to her house to get George's gun. But once she had it in her hands, she realized she could never shoot anyone and left it there in George's desk."

My gaze zeroed in on Happy. "You knew about this?"

She shook her head. "I dropped her off in town while I ran to the post office. When I picked her up, we drove over to the house to pick up a few things. She never said anything about a gun, or I wouldn't have driven her over there. As clumsy as she is, she'd probably shoot off her own foot."

"Did Lula Mae tell you she was staying with us the night Percy was murdered?" I asked, trying to be helpful.

He regarded me gravely. "Are you prepared to testify she was never out of your sight the entire evening? That she didn't slip out of the house for a rendezvous with her boyfriend, or go back to her place to make sure she hadn't left the stove on?"

"Well, no." I stumbled over the words. "I was on a date that night, but Happy was here. I'm sure she can vouch for her."

He turned to Happy. "How about it? Did you see your sister between the hours of say nine and midnight? Maybe run into her on your way to the bathroom, or share a snack with her in the kitchen?"

Happy shook her head. "I zonked out the minute my head

hit the pillow. But you can take my word for it, Lula Mae wouldn't kill anyone. Not even that louse, Percy Moss, who deserved it. Why, the man paraded all over town like he was some kind of saint, when all the time he was—"

"Your trust in your sister's innocence is very touching," he said. "But I'm afraid we're going to need more than your word to back up her story."

We sat down with him and, for the next hour, went over every conceivable thing we could think of that might have some bearing on Lula Mae's case. When we were done, Sam snapped his briefcase shut. "That about does it."

Once he was gone, we finally got around to having some lunch. Well, I had lunch; Happy only poked at hers.

Finally, she gave up any pretense of eating. "What do you think Lula Mae's chances are of beating this thing?"

I swallowed a mouthful of chocolate chip cookie and washed it down with a gulp of milk before answering. "The police seem to be building a good case against her. Unless we come up with the killer's identity, I think her chances are looking pretty slim."

"I can't believe it's come to this." Happy shook her head sadly.

While we sat there, pondering Lula Mae's fate, the doorbell rang. "Who in blazes could that be?" I wiped my hands on a napkin and, with Happy glued to my heels, went to answer it.

I opened the door to find Mrs. Mayfield standing there, looking as if she'd been stung by a passel of bees. Her face was all red and splotchy and puffed up like a balloon.

"I'm so sorry to show up on your doorstep like this." She dabbed at her eyes with a lace-edged handkerchief. "But I didn't know where else to go."

I wasn't good at dealing with emotional women, so I stepped aside and let Happy take over. "Don't be silly," Happy said, slipping an arm around the woman's shoulders. "You're not bothering us. Come sit down and tell us what's wrong."

As Happy led our guest toward the living room, I muttered something about putting on a pot of tea and disappeared into the kitchen. Ten minutes later, I joined them, carrying a tray with three cups of hot tea and a platter of Happy's chocolate chip cookies. Praying that my klutzy gene didn't kick in, I carefully lowered Grandma Rose's silver tray to the coffee table.

"Thank you, dear." Mrs. Mayfield accepted the cup of tea I held out to her and took a sip. "Ah, Orange Spice," she noted, before settling back against the cushions. "I was just telling your mother what a shock it was to read about Percy's death in the newspaper. I mean, to open up the newspaper and see his face staring back at me." She was back to dabbing at her eyes.

"I'm sure it must have been . . . devastating." I tried for that soothing tone that always worked so well for Happy. "Especially considering how close the two of you were." Something must have been missing in my technique because the trickle of tears rolling down her face increased.

"Vivian was just telling me," Happy said, reaching over to pat Mrs. Mayfield's hand, "that she's spent the last few days taking care of her next-door neighbor, Mary Ellen. The poor thing has had a stomach virus."

In other words, Mrs. Mayfield has an alibi for Saturday evening. "I'm sorry about your friend," I said. "Too bad you had to spend such a lovely weekend stuck inside taking care of her."

"Oh, I didn't mind. Last year when I had that bad case of shingles, Mary Ellen stayed right by my side, fixing my meals, dishing out my pain medicine. I simply returned the favor."

Happy looked puzzled. "Vivian, I know you read about Percy's death in the newspaper, but that doesn't explain how you found us. Our address certainly wasn't in the paper."

Mrs. Mayfield reached inside her purse and pulled out one of our business cards. "Where did you get that?" Happy asked, her gaze shifting to me.

I held up my hands in mock surrender. "Guilty as charged."

"To be honest, dear, I couldn't find the card you gave me. This one"—she stuffed it back into her purse—"is the one Lula Mae gave me."

Happy's eyebrows knotted, scrolling through her memory for the incident.

"I think you were in the bathroom at the time," Mrs. Mayfield said. "Poor thing. She was so worried about Percy. She made me promise to call her the minute I heard from him. When she didn't answer her phone, I called the garden center and that nice young girl you have working for you told me where I could find you."

Good thing Mrs. Mayfield was some harmless old lady and not our killer; otherwise, we might be fish bait by now.

"I heard on the TV the police suspect Lula Mae of killing him," Mrs. Mayfield went on. "I don't believe it. Lula Mae is such a sweetheart. She doesn't have a mean bone in her body."

Happy snorted. "You'd understand if you'd met some of the policemen in this town. Complete idiots, the bunch of them. Why, most of them are nothing but kids."

"Hey," I warned.

"My daughter here," Happy said, motioning toward me with a disgusted look on her face, "is even dating one of them."

Mrs. Mayfield leaned back, a shocked look in her eyes.

"I plead temporary insanity," I said in my defense.

"I should hope so," she said. "Especially after the way they've been treating your aunt."

"I think the girl's coming to her senses," Happy went on, "now that she sees what kind of man he is."

"That reminds me," Mrs. Mayfield said, "some policeman came around my place a few days ago asking lots of questions about Percy. The way the man was carrying on, you would've thought he was on the FBI's most wanted list."

"You don't say." Happy's nose for gossip perked up. "What kinds of questions did he ask?"

Mrs. Mayfield took another sip of tea before answering. "He mainly wanted to know about any investments I'd made based on Percy's advice. When I told him that it was none of his business how I spent my money, he got downright testy. But for the life of me, I can't figure out how he knew about me. I don't even live in this town."

I snatched another cookie off the platter, and tried not to look guilty. "Is that all he wanted to know?"

Her forehead wrinkled. "He also asked me about some woman who'd died recently. I can't seem to recall her name at the moment."

"Camilla Davenport?" I suggested.

She nodded. "That sounds right. I told him I'd read about her death in the newspaper, but I'd never met the woman." She placed a hand over her throat. "He even asked me my whereabouts during what I assume was the time of her murder. Why, I've never been so humiliated in all my life."

"I wouldn't take it personally. That's pretty much the way the police are treating Lula Mae," Happy said.

"Well, I've taken up enough of your time." Mrs. Mayfield struggled to her feet. "I'd best be going."

Happy and I walked her to the door. Before leaving, she turned and gave Happy a hug. "I'm sure the police will find the person who killed Percy soon, and Lula Mae will be home again, safe and sound. In the meantime, please accept my condolences for your loss. And do give me a call when you've completed your brother's funeral arrangements."

"Percy's not—" Happy began.

I gave her a jab in the ribs. "I'll make sure someone calls

219

you," I said.

"You didn't have to be so rough," Happy complained as Mrs. Mayfield climbed into her car. "I'm an old woman. My side's liable to ache for a month."

"You were about to tell her that Percy wasn't your brother."

"Well, he's not."

"Yes, but when I went by her place, I told her I was looking for my uncle. How do you think she's going to feel when she finds out Lula Mae was Percy's fiancée?"

Happy sighed. "Not too well, I'm afraid."

CHAPTER THIRTY-EIGHT

A few minutes later, Happy complained about a headache and went upstairs to lie down. I decided to head next door and see how things were going at the garden center.

Not too well, it appeared. There were exactly two cars in the parking lot, Jolene's MG and a silver Lexus. Hopefully, this was only a temporary lull in business; otherwise, we might not be able to afford Sam's services.

As I drew near the office, I heard Jolene's agitated voice coming from inside. "Maybe you should get out of town until things settle down."

I hesitated outside the door, debating whether to burst inside and find out what had Jolene so riled up, or stay where I was and let her handle the situation on her own.

"You know I can't do that," Keith said.

"I could come with you," Jolene offered.

"No." Keith must have realized how harsh he sounded, for he went on to add more gently, "Look, honey, I know you want to help, but you're in this deep enough already. I don't want anything to happen to you because of my mistakes."

What mistakes? I wanted to shout.

"But I love you." There was a note of desperation in her voice. "There must be something I can do."

"Look, sweetheart," he said, "I appreciate your wanting to help, but the stakes are getting higher, especially with that Spencer broad breathing down my neck."

"I'm not a broad," I muttered, feeling my temper start to rise.

"Don't worry about Kate," she told him. "I can take care of her."

"I don't want you to take care of anything. This is my problem, not yours. I don't want you involved in any of this. Understand?"

"Okay," she reluctantly agreed. "But remember, I'm here if you need me."

"I appreciate your support, babe. But after tonight, I figure our troubles will be over."

My mind flew in a million directions. Something, evidently, was in the works for tonight, but what? Not another murder, I hoped.

A few minutes later, Keith came waltzing out the door. I barely had time to duck around the corner. I waited until I heard his car start up, then strolled inside. "Hey, Jolene, how are things going?"

"Okay, I guess." She was busy stacking Styrofoam cups next to the coffeepot. "You'll be happy to know the preacher's wife came in earlier with a couple of her buddies. Seems they've decided to put in a water garden by the fellowship hall. They bought oodles of stuff."

"Great. I'll be sure to mention it to Happy. She'll be thrilled her idea is bringing in so much business." I tried to find a way to broach the subject of Keith without making her think I was butting into her business. "I thought I saw your boyfriend pulling out of the parking lot just now," was the best I could come up with.

"So?" Her tone was defensive.

"So, nothing. I was just making conversation."

Jolene pulled out the plastic liner in the trashcan and proceeded to tie the top into a knot. I unrolled a new liner and tucked it into the can. "I guess you've heard by now that the police have arrested Lula Mae for Percy's murder."

"I heard." She set the trash bag aside and dumped more packets of sweetener into the bowl next to the coffeepot.

"You know Lula Mae pretty well." I studied her face closely. "Do you think she's capable of murder?"

She shrugged. "The way I hear it, most people are murdered by someone they know. That certainly fits in Lula Mae's case. She *was* the man's fiancée."

I was appalled by what I was hearing, even though I shouldn't have been. Especially after overhearing her conversation with Keith. My best guess was, Jolene was looking for someone to blame. Someone besides Keith. "I can't believe you said that. You of all people know what a soft heart Lula Mae has."

"The police must be pretty certain about her guilt. Why else would they have arrested her?"

"Lula Mae would never kill anyone," I repeated, more forcefully. "Besides, what possible reason would she have had for wanting Percy dead?"

"How about jealousy or revenge. How's that for starters?"

I decided it was time to make a few insinuations of my own. "We both know there are other people in this town with stronger motives for wanting Percy dead."

"Name one." Her eyes warned me that I'd better not say Keith Davenport.

"Stella Barnes, for one."

"Who?" She looked surprised. "What's Stella got to do with this?"

"You wanted to know someone with a motive. Stella Barnes. She has a motive. She gave Percy a large sum of money to buy bakery equipment. When she realized he never had any intention of buying equipment . . . well, I'd say that was motive enough for murder."

The gears were turning in her brain. "But how does that fit with Camilla's murder?"

"Because Stella was engaged to Percy Moss, and Camilla was trying to steal him from her."

Why did that statement sound so familiar?

Jolene's brow furrowed. "But I thought Lula Mae was engaged to Percy."

"It's a long story." I waved a hand in the air. "I don't have time to go into all the details now. The thing is, there are lots of other people who had a motive to kill both Camilla and Percy."

"Just because Stella was angry at Percy," Jolene pointed out, "it doesn't mean she killed him."

I smiled. "Exactly."

Realizing she'd been tricked, Jolene grumbled, "I guess you have a point."

On a roll, I went on, "Since we both agree it's unlikely that Lula Mae killed anyone—that means someone else did."

She stiffened. "I know where you're headed with this, and I don't like it one bit."

I dredged up my most innocent expression. "I don't have the slightest idea what you're talking about."

"Don't play games with me. Keith told me how you've been badgering him and his brother about their mother's death."

"If he's innocent, then—"

"*If* he's innocent." She kicked the garbage can near her feet. "You have a lot of nerve; you know that? Lula Mae's been hauled down to the police station twice, and here you are questioning my boyfriend's innocence. Maybe you should take care of the problems in your own backyard before you go blaming others."

"What do you think I'm doing? I know Lula Mae didn't kill Camilla. Or Percy. And I intend to prove it."

"Well, Keith didn't kill anybody either. And nobody had better go around saying he did, or bad things are liable to happen."

That sounded like a threat. "What kinds of bad things?"

She snatched up the garbage bag. "Just keep your nose out of other people's business and you won't have anything to worry about."

CHAPTER THIRTY-NINE

After her bail hearing, Lula Mae was soon back in the folds of her family. "You have no idea how horrible that place was. I was surrounded by nothing but heathens. I was mighty lucky to get out of there alive."

"I know, hon." Happy seemed delighted to resume the role of big sister. She gave Lula Mae a mild sedative, then ushered her upstairs to rest.

"You ought to take one of those things yourself," I told her when she returned. "You look half dead."

"You don't look so hot yourself."

"Touché," I said.

"Don't go using those foreign words with me, young lady. How many times have I told you—"

I tuned out the rest of her babbling and went back to watching TV. At least the main character, unlike some people in the room, had the decency to treat his daughter like an adult. After things were neatly wrapped up on the show, I got up and switched off the set.

Happy sighed. "If only Lula Mae's problems could be solved in sixty minutes."

I gave her an encouraging smile. "I have a feeling Lula Mae's situation is going to improve soon."

"Have you got some crystal ball up in your room I don't know about?"

It frightened me to see her so discouraged, so I tried to

comfort her the same way she had always comforted me. I offered her food. "How about a dish of ice cream?"

She nodded, then followed me into the kitchen and sagged down in chair while I filled two bowls with chocolate chip ice cream. "I guess we'd better check out Vivian's alibi tomorrow."

"You don't believe she was taking care of her sick friend?"

She shrugged. "People lie. And with Lula Mae's life at stake, we can't afford to take any chances."

"I don't think she knew about Lula Mae and Percy's engagement. Or Stella and Percy's engagement."

Happy looked thoughtful. "You suppose that no-good bum talked Vivian into giving him money to open that stupid bakery?"

"Yep." I sat her bowl of ice cream on the table, then slid into the chair across from her. "She gave him five thousand dollars, just like Stella."

Happy's eyebrows flew up. "That much?" She poked at her ice cream with her spoon. "You think he ever had any intention of starting a bakery?"

"When alligators fly."

She sighed. "That's what I thought." Her eyes narrowed. "Remember the night you gave that class on container water gardening, how I told you how this Lula Mae–Percy relationship was headed for trouble?"

"I remember all right." And wished now I had taken her more seriously. "Want a brownie to go with your ice cream?"

She ignored my question. "You think Sam can get Lula Mae out of this mess?"

"Absolutely."

She eyed me speculatively. The way mothers do when they're trying to decide if one of their offspring is up to something. "What are you hiding?"

I scooped the last bit of ice cream into my mouth and headed to the sink with my bowl. "Where's all that faith when you need it?"

Happy joined me at the sink. "You didn't answer my question."

Hoping to drown out her words, I turned the water on full force. But like a dog with a chew toy, she wouldn't let go. "I know you're up to something, young lady. Best just spill your guts and get it over with."

Realizing I had to give her something, I said, "Let's just say that I'm working on an idea that might clear up a lot of things."

"Such as?"

"I'll explain it all tomorrow. When Lula Mae's awake. That way I won't have to repeat myself."

Happy didn't like it, but she let me have this one. Temporarily, at least.

When Happy was safely tucked away in bed, I let myself out the front door. The night air was still warm, and there was a full moon overhead. As my truck engine rumbled to life, I darted a glance toward the house, praying Happy wouldn't suddenly appear and demand an explanation.

When no flaming redhead popped up in the window, I relaxed, pressed down on the accelerator, and set off for the lake, determined to get some answers.

Keith's place wasn't hard to spot. It was the only one with a silver Lexus parked in front. I passed it by, moseyed on down the road, and scanned the area for signs of activity. Didn't notice any. Turned around and headed back in the direction of Keith's cabin.

The cabin across from his appeared to be vacant. Dousing the lights, I puttered down the gravel drive and swung around at the end to face the road.

From here I had a pretty good view of the squat, rustic building Keith had rented. Along one end, lights blazed. The main living area, I figured. The rest of the place was shrouded in darkness.

I sat there for what seemed like days, but in reality was probably only a few hours. Occasionally, a curtain would move and I'd catch a glimpse of someone peering out. But other than that, all was quiet.

I don't know what I'd expected, but this was definitely not my idea of getting to the bottom of things. So far, I'd been serenaded by a handful of frogs and an army of crickets, then eaten alive by bear-sized mosquitoes.

I was getting ready to pack it in when I noticed a white Mercedes tooling down the road. The car slowed, then swung in next to the Lexus. The porch light flashed on. Seconds later, the cabin door flew open and Keith stepped outside.

A tall, slender figure in black emerged from the Mercedes and approached the door. Light bouncing off the pale mass of hair left little doubt to his visitor's identity. Evelyn Davenport. The question was, what was she doing here?

There was only one way to find out. As soon as the front door closed behind her, I shot out of the truck and trotted across the road. Between the moonlight and all the security lights, I could see where I was going well enough.

When I reached the cabin, I scooted past the jungle of rosebushes some idiot had planted too close to the building, and made my way to the window. A narrow gap between the curtain panels gave me a good view of the interior.

Not that there was much to look at inside: a couple of chairs, a couch, and a bookcase. All of it thrift-store quality. The most expensive item in the room was the TV set, which probably hadn't been part of the cabin's decor at all, but was something that belonged to Keith personally. I didn't see any sign of Jolene. I guess she'd decided to honor his wishes and had stayed home.

"What's this about?" Evelyn asked, not bothering with formalities. "You sounded so mysterious on the phone. I have better things to do with my time than—"

"It's about the truth," Keith broke in.

Evelyn sank down on the ratty couch. "The truth comes in many flavors, dear brother-in-law. Which particular flavor interests you?"

Keith slid into the chair across from her. "The one that explains why you killed my mother."

"You've got to be kidding." She sounded incredulous.

"Don't play games with me." His voice hardened. "I did a little checking. I know you were in town the night Mother was murdered."

Evelyn's laughter rang out, loud and cold. "You're delusional. I was nowhere near Port Springs the night your mother was killed. I was in New Orleans. At my best friend's wedding."

"Is that so? I talked to a few people who were at your friend Cynthia's wedding. They remember seeing you at the wedding, but not at the reception."

"They were probably too drunk to remember where they were, much less who they saw."

"What about this?" He reached into the shopping bag beside his chair and pulled out a bright orange scarf. "I found it in the kitchen when the police let us back in the house. They probably assumed it belonged to Mother, but I know it wasn't hers."

He wadded up the scarf and tossed it in her direction. She caught it with one hand and let it drop into her lap. "Recognize it?" he asked.

Without bothering to examine it, she said, "Can't say that I do."

"That's funny," he said, "since it belongs to you."

"Who made you the expert on my wardrobe?"

"It's not Mother's. Believe me, I know. I once gave her an

230

orange sweater for her birthday and she quickly informed me that orange was not her color. And in the future, if I wanted to give her clothes, I should consider a gift certificate instead."

"All that proves is that you have bad taste in fashion. But don't feel bad, most men seem to have that problem. It's in their genes."

He pushed on. "Want to tell me how it got there? You and Tony haven't been to Mother's place since Christmas."

"I'm sure you're not familiar with every item of clothing in your mother's wardrobe. How do you know someone didn't give it to her for her birthday? Someone who didn't know about her aversion to the color orange." She paused a moment, then went on, "Or maybe it belongs to one of those busybody friends of hers."

"Remember that trip you and Tony took to the mountains last year?" He grabbed a photo album off the coffee table, opened it, then held it out to her. "Recognize the scarf?"

"So I own a scarf like your mother's." She started to rise. "If that's all you've got."

"There's more." He reached into the shopping bag again and pulled out a black velvet pouch, then slid the contents onto the coffee table. Light danced off what looked like . . . jewelry.

The color drained from her face. Then she rallied, tilted up her chin, and said, "What did you do, ransack Barbara's jewelry box? You think that necklace and earrings"—she swept out a hand to indicate the pieces spread out on the table—"will make that little floozy down at the Flower Patch happy?"

"Come on. You can do better than that. I'm sure you've seen Mother wear these pieces often enough."

Her composure didn't slip. "I heard the cops found some of your mother's jewelry in that Lulu woman's car. Did they return it already?"

"You and I both know that Lula Mae Elkins had nothing to

do with Mother's murder."

She snorted. "Get real. Your mother and this woman have been fighting over men for years."

"Yet neither one of them ever resorted to murder."

"Until now." Evelyn smiled, then laid out her scenario. "My guess is this Lulu woman finally got fed up with your mother for trying to steal her man. They fought. Things got out of hand. Lulu snatched up one of the fireplace pokers and put an end to your mother's interference, once and for all."

"Lula Mae is an old woman. I doubt she has the strength to—"

"Don't underestimate the woman because of her age," Evelyn said. "People do all sorts of things when they're enraged. Things they couldn't ordinarily do."

"Are you speaking from experience?"

She ignored his question. "Face it, this Lulu woman had the best reason in the world to want your mother dead. If someone stole my man, I might be tempted to bash her head in, too."

"That old killer instinct at work, right?"

She sat up a little straighter. "I believe in going after what I want. Nothing wrong with that."

He shook his head in disbelief. "How do you think Tony's going to feel when he finds out what you did to our mother?"

"Like I told you," she said, "I didn't do anything."

He nodded at the items on the coffee table. "I'm sure the man at the pawn shop will be happy to testify about the nice-looking blonde who brought these pieces in."

"Okay." Evelyn gave up the pretense. "So maybe I pawned some of your mother's stuff. That doesn't mean I killed her."

He scooted forward in his chair. "How much more of Mother's jewelry did you steal? Should I be checking out more pawn shops?"

"I didn't steal any of your mother's jewelry." Evelyn crossed her arms and glared at him. "She gave me those pieces."

He snorted. "You don't really expect me to believe that."

"I don't really care what you believe," she said. "Ever since your dad died, your mother almost never went anywhere. All that stuff was just sitting in her jewelry box, collecting dust. So she decided to pass along some of it. An early inheritance, you might say."

"Yeah, right."

"Your mother *gave* those pieces to me," she insisted.

There was a long silence, then he said, "So, tell me, how did the jewelry Mother *gave* you end up in that pawn shop in New Orleans?"

She swept back a lock of hair. "Oh, for goodness sakes, none of that stuff"—she inclined her head toward the coffee table—"is really my style."

"Right." He sounded skeptical.

"Okay. So I sold a few pieces of your mother's jewelry. Big deal. It's not like she didn't have plenty more. The old biddy knew Tony and I were having some financial difficulties. If she'd given us the loan we asked for, I wouldn't have had to pawn any of her stupid old stuff."

"Stuff she gave to you?" he reiterated.

She stuck to her story. "That's what I said."

"I wonder if the police will buy that."

After a long silence, Evelyn said, "Look, Tony and I can afford to be generous. What do you want? Money? Our portion of your mother's house?"

He shook his head. "That would be too easy. I want you to pay for killing my mother."

She gave a mirthless laugh. "That's not going to happen. Face it, I did you the biggest favor of your life. With the money you get from Camilla's estate, you can afford to pay off that wife of yours and marry your little floozy."

"You think money is the only thing that matters?"

"Quite frankly, yes, I do. And I'm sure it means something to your girlfriend. It's time for you to grow up and face the facts. Your mother was a mean, selfish woman who used money to control everyone around her, including you, dear brother-in-law. Whether you care to admit it or not."

"Granted, my mother was no saint," he said, "but she didn't deserve to die before her time."

"That depends on what side of the fence you're sitting on."

He shook his head in disbelief. "You really are heartless. At least my mother loved her family. She'd never—"

"Spare me the sermon. I've already heard quite enough from that imbecile preacher about what a good person Camilla was. All the wonderful things she did for the community. But the truth is, your mother was a rotten, conniving woman who killed people every day of her life. Not with bullets, but with money. She alone had the power to decide whose dreams lived, and whose died."

Keith stood up. "You can't blame Mother because Davenport Hardware was on the verge of bankruptcy. That was your own doing."

"Funny, that's just how she put it. According to her, I spent too much money. I didn't have the right personality to deal with the public. I undermined her son at every opportunity."

"She had a valid point. Look how much money you've spent in the last few days. Enough to feed a family of four for a year, I'd say."

Too worked up to sit still any longer, Evelyn leaped to her feet and began to prowl around the room. "What none of you seem to realize is, I'm the one who's kept the business going all these years."

She stalked toward the window, forcing me to duck out of sight. I held my breath and prayed she couldn't hear the hammering going on inside my chest.

Realizing he wasn't responding the way she wanted, Evelyn tried a new tactic. "Did you know your mother offered Barbara a hundred thousand dollars to drop the divorce?"

"Mother would never—"

"Bribe her own daughter-in-law?" She moved away from the window. "Don't be so naïve. Your mother would've made a deal with the devil if it got her what she wanted."

I risked another look inside.

In the past few moments, Keith seemed to have visibly aged. Gone was the confident man-of-the-world. "You're lying." His shoulders sagged. "Mother wouldn't . . . what possible reason would she have to do something like that?"

Evelyn gave a snort. "That's easy. She wanted to save you from the clutches of that floozy down at the garden store."

Reality was beginning to kick in. "That's ridiculous. Jolene is the best thing that's ever happened to me. We're happy together."

"Too bad your mother didn't see it that way."

He shook his head in disgust. "You're some piece of work, you know that?"

She shrugged. "What can I say? It's a gift from God."

"That gift's not going to do you much good behind bars." He grabbed his cell phone off the coffee table and began to punch in numbers.

Evelyn calmly reached into her handbag and pulled out a gun. "I suggest you sit down and hand me that phone."

"And if I don't?"

"Then we'll see if that heart of yours is bulletproof."

He stood there a moment, weighing his decision. "You can't seriously expect to get away with another murder."

"You'd be surprised by what I can get away with."

He seemed to realize his options were limited. He tossed the phone on the table, then slumped down in his chair.

"Good decision." Evelyn swept up the phone with one hand and deposited it in her purse. "Now maybe we put our heads together and come up with a solution we can both live with."

CHAPTER FORTY

Deciding this might be a good time to go for help, I eased away from the window. And ran smack dab into one of the rosebushes, which hugged the house. A soft moan escaped my lips as thorns ripped into tender flesh. I shot a look back toward the window, prayed I wouldn't see psycho woman's face.

So far, so good.

While I was busy prying my blouse loose from the prickly thorns, I heard what sounded like a scuffle taking place inside. In one swift motion, I ripped my blouse free and raced back to the window. This time, I didn't worry about being seen, but plastered my face right up against the pane.

What I saw made my blood freeze.

Evelyn and Keith were fighting for control of the gun. Since Keith was larger and stronger, he appeared to have the upper hand. But he was no match for Evelyn's tenacity. In one quick motion, she rammed her knee into his crotch. He groaned, then let go of the gun and doubled over.

With an evil grin on her face, she moved in, slammed the gun down on his head, then stepped out of the way as he fell forward, slamming headfirst into the hard wooden floor. To make sure he stayed down, she whipped out a pair of zip ties and cuffed his wrists and ankles.

I held my breath, willing him to wake up. When he made no effort to comply, a cry of alarm escaped my lips. Like an eagle zooming in on her prey, Evelyn whirled around, her eyes searching for the source of the disturbance.

My heart went wild. I darted out of sight, plastering my body against the rough cypress siding. A moment later, the curtains snapped open. An eternity seemed to pass before they fell back into place. Wishing I hadn't been so closed-minded about owning a cell phone, I inched around the thorny landscaping and took off running.

As I sailed past the front porch, the door flew open. Seconds later, a shot rang out.

Believe me, I didn't stand around like some dumb chicken waiting to be plucked off. Adrenaline plunged through my body, making my legs pump harder. I was almost to the road when a second shot whizzed past me.

Yelling for me to stop, Evelyn charged after me. My mama didn't raise no fool. I kept right on running.

She fired a third shot.

My guardian angel must have been working overtime because the bullet only grazed my shoulder, doing no serious damage. Thankfully, I was so high on adrenaline, I didn't feel any pain. But what had seemed like a short trot over, now seemed to stretch into infinity. My chest began to ache from the effort it took to suck in a breath.

Just when I thought my legs were going to collapse, I reached my truck and plowed inside. My hands were shaking so badly it took several tries to get the keys out of my pocket and into the ignition. Muttering a quick prayer, I gunned the engine. Gravel spewed in all directions as I shot down the drive.

Evelyn moved to block my path, the gun thrust out in front of her in a shooter's stance. The scene struck me as surreal. Like stepping into some B-rated movie. "You might as well give up," she yelled. "There's no way you're getting past me."

"Oh, yeah?" I jerked the wheel hard to the left and took off across the grass toward the road. Even though it hadn't rained in weeks, the ground was soggy in places and several times I almost bogged up in the soft earth.

With Evelyn hot on my heels, I had no choice but to keep going. When I reached the ditch, my luck ran out. Instead of the shallow depression I expected, a virtual gully was buried beneath that tangle of elephant ears. My front wheels pitched smoothly into the air, then sank.

My head slammed into the steering column, giving me one heck of a headache to go with the dull ache I was beginning to feel in my shoulder. With shaking hands, I opened the door and tried to climb out. But Evelyn was already on me. "Get out," she ordered, pointing her gun at my head.

Since I couldn't come up with any safe option, I did as she ordered, climbing out of the cab and sinking almost up to my waist in the swampy vegetation. I darted a look around, hoping no water moccasins were slithering about in the murky water, ready to strike.

"Don't try anything foolish," Evelyn warned. "Keep your hands where I can see them."

The thought of rushing her flicked through my mind, followed by the realization that Keith had already been down that path, and look where it had gotten him.

"Let's go." She motioned toward Keith's cabin with the gun. "You've been nothing but trouble since the day I met you. Now I have no choice, but to make sure you and my dear brother-in-law share the same fate."

As she herded me across the street, I blurted out the question that had been burning inside me. "Just tell me one thing. Why did you do it?"

She seemed surprised by the question. "For the money, of course."

"If you'd just asked Camilla, I'm sure she would've given you all the money you needed."

"As I'm sure you overheard, I already tried that. I all but got down on my hands and knees and begged her. But all that witch did was laugh in my face. Said it was my love for luxuries that had gotten us into this mess in the first place."

I looked back over my shoulder. "I'm sure Tony could've found a way to convince her."

Her eyes narrowed. "Tony didn't have the guts to even ask her. He'd prefer to stand by and watch all our hard work go down the drain."

"But you had enough guts for both of you?" I phrased it as a question.

"Who else was there? From the beginning, I've been the one who kept things going. I was the one everyone came to with their problems. Tony was nothing more than a figurehead. He got all the glory, while I did all the work."

My shoulder was really aching now. Blood leaked down my arm. But I couldn't give in to the pain; I still needed answers. "Why drag Percy and Lula Mae into the middle of things? You could've just made Camilla's death seem like a robbery gone bad."

"If I'd been given a choice, I wouldn't have involved them. It only made things more complicated."

We were almost to the cabin now. "So what changed your mind?" I asked, as she moved up beside me.

"That little weasel, Percy, was hiding in the other room when I tried to persuade Camilla to give us the money. He heard everything."

"And tried to blackmail you," I guessed.

A sly smile touched her lips. "Let's just say, he expected to walk away from our meeting at Lula Mae's considerably richer."

Arriving at our destination, Evelyn motioned toward Camilla's car. "You and I are taking a little trip."

"What about Keith?" I asked, darting a look toward the cabin.

She flashed me a smug grin. "I don't think he'll be going anywhere soon."

What did that say about my own chances for survival?

My only hope was to keep her talking and wait for a chance to escape. "Where are we going?"

She thought about it a minute. "The way I figure it, I've got to come up with a story that will logically explain your death. Like"—she snapped her fingers—"that robbery gone bad idea you mentioned."

"Come on. Nobody's going to buy that."

Her cold, green eyes settled on me. "Don't count on it. By the time I'm done, the police won't find any evidence your death was anything but a robbery."

"And Keith's death? Is that going to look like another robbery gone bad?"

"I haven't figured that part out yet," she said. "But I will. It seems I have a real talent for murder." Looking into her eyes, I saw no guilt, no remorse. And I knew her words were true.

She motioned toward Camilla's car and told me to get in. For once, I did the sensible thing and did as I was told. Steven would be real proud of me. Not that he was ever going to know it.

Ever vigilant, Evelyn kept the gun aimed somewhere in the vicinity of my chest as she crawled in beside me. She dug the keys out of her pocket and tossed them to me. "Time to head over to the garden center and take care of business."

We drove along in silence for several minutes, then my curiosity prompted me to ask, "What I don't get is how you managed to sneak into town without anyone noticing."

"Easy." She seemed almost eager to share her cleverness, which I didn't think was a good sign for my future. "I had to fly into New Orleans for a friend's wedding. During the festivities I . . . borrowed . . . a car, took care of my business with Camilla, then got back in time to party with some of the other guests."

"I can't believe the police bought that alibi. New Orleans is not that far away. They should've realized you had time to drive to Camilla's, kill her, and get back in time for breakfast."

"Except the police have a witness that places me at the reception, then at one of the local bars until the wee hours of the morning."

"How did you manage that?"

That evil smile was back. "Easy. I cuddled up to some old guy I met at the wedding, who'd had a little too much to drink. It wasn't hard to convince him we'd been together all evening. I even had the foresight to get one of his business cards so the police could contact him."

Unbelievable. "He must have been stone cold drunk."

"Pretty close to it."

When we reached the Flower Patch, Evelyn ordered me to turn in. At this time of night, the place was deserted. Hoping to project an air of confidence as we walked through the gate— which Happy was supposed to have locked when we'd closed up, but apparently hadn't—I said, "You do realize that you can't get away with killing me." I nodded toward the house perched on the lot next door. "All I have to do is yell and Happy and Lula Mae will come running."

"I'm sure you don't want to put their lives in danger."

I was getting desperate. "Anybody driving by can see the light on in the office."

"I'm counting on it." She sounded so matter-of-fact. "Some crazed junkie was in the neighborhood, saw the lights on, and figured he could get money for his next fix."

"We never leave money in the register overnight," I said smugly.

She didn't seem too concerned by such a minor detail. "Too bad he didn't know that."

She prodded me in the ribs with the barrel of her gun. "I don't have all night. Get over there and open the door. And be quick about it."

I took great pleasure in pointing out that my keys were still in my truck, which was back at Keith's place.

"I'm sure you must have a spare around here. Find it, or I won't hesitate to use this." She pressed the gun in my back to emphasize her point.

There was no doubt in my mind she would pull the trigger. I reached under the pot of marigolds beside the door and retrieved the key. By then, my hands were shaking so hard, I had trouble fitting it in the lock.

Foolish thoughts began to race through my head. Like, maybe I could rush inside and slam the door in her face. Or I could wait until we got inside, then make a dash for the phone. Better yet, I could quit being such a coward and knock the gun right out of her hand.

There was only one problem with all those ideas. They could get me killed.

As soon as I got the door unlocked, Evelyn herded me inside. "Open the register."

Glad to put as much distance between us as possible, I scooted around the pile of flowerpots at the end of the counter and popped open the register. Once again, I tried to make her understand how foolish her plan was. "I'm sure the police have gotten calls by now about the gunfire out by the lake. They'll be able to match any bullets recovered to the scene here."

"Doesn't matter," she said. "I plan to leave the gun behind. They'll trace it back to Percy."

"How'd you wind up with his gun?"

She smiled. "I took it off him. Right after I lured him out to the lake."

"Why would he meet you?" I asked. "What did you have that

he wanted?"

She looked at me as if I were an imbecile. "Money, of course." She paused a beat. "Of course, he had no idea I'd planted Camilla's diamond necklace in the glove compartment of his car so the police would connect him to her murder. The idiot was supposed to stay put until the police checked out an anonymous tip."

I tried to take advantage of her talking spree. "Since you'd already connected Percy to Camilla's death, why put those earrings in my aunt's car?"

"To confuse the police." She chuckled. "You do realize they're nothing but bumbling idiots."

A slight movement outside the window caught my attention. "I don't think you'd be stupid enough to kill me in front of a witness." I nodded toward the open door.

"You can't think I'm stupid enough to fall for that ploy." She sounded amused.

"What ploy?" a voice came from the doorway.

As Evelyn swung around to confront Happy, I snatched up one of the flowerpots near the counter and slammed it down on her head. She sank to the floor in a heap.

Happy rushed over. "What'd you do that for? She's liable to sue us."

"Are you blind?" I darted over and kicked the gun away from Evelyn's body. It sailed across the room and landed under a seed display in the corner. "Couldn't you see that she was trying to kill me?"

Happy stood there with a shocked expression on her face, while I put in a call to the police. After telling them what happened, I added, "And get an ambulance out to the cabins by the lake. The one with a silver Lexus parked in front. A man's been injured."

By the time I got off the phone, Lula Mae had loped inside

the office to join us. "What's going on out here?"

As I filled her in on the night's events, Evelyn began to stir. Happy hurried over and snatched up a shovel from the tool rack. "Don't you move, missy," she told Evelyn, "or I'll give you a good dose of Spencer medicine you won't soon forget."

"That's not fair," Lula Mae began to whine. "You always get to do all the fun stuff. Here"—she tried to snatch the shovel away—"give me a turn."

Nipping that idea, I reached over and forcefully removed the shovel from Happy's grip. "Neither one of you is going to be passing out any medicine. The police should be here any minute. They can take care of dispensing any medicine that's needed."

As if waiting offstage for their cue, the wail of sirens split the air, followed seconds later by a passel of police cars whipping into the parking lot. Soon a whole herd of policemen came dashing through the door. And on their heels, came Steven.

"I never thought I'd actually be glad to see you," Happy said. She pointed a bony finger at Evelyn. "Arrest that woman. She tried to kill my baby girl."

Lula Mae frowned. "I've told you a million times. She isn't your baby anymore. And the poor boy did come running to her rescue. Maybe you should give him a chance."

"Oh, hush up," Happy snapped. "Weren't you the one who suggested we boil him in oil last night?"

"That's only because he accused me of killing Percy." Lula Mae tilted her nose in the air. "I've mellowed since then."

Steven turned to me seeking a rational explanation for Evelyn's presence on the floor. As soon as I told him my story, he started issuing instructions to his men. "By the way," Steven said when he got back, "looks like Keith might just make it."

As Evelyn was hauled outside, she looked at me and began to yell, "You just got lucky this time, but I'll get you for this. You hear me? I'll make sure you pay for what you've done to me."

"Get her out of here," Steven ordered. When she was gone, he turned to me. Gave me the "look." The one that says, you've done something really stupid. "You realize you could have gotten yourself killed tonight?"

My dander started to rise. "But I didn't."

"But you could have." That stubborn jaw of his poked out a mile.

"But I didn't."

Coming up behind him, Lula Mae said, "Oh, just kiss the girl and be done with it."

A twinkle lit his eyes. "That's sounds like a good idea," he said. Then proceeded to do just that.

Behind his back, the speculations began. "How soon do you think it'll be before they get married?" Lula Mae wanted to know.

"I'd give them a couple of months," Happy said. "Three at the most."

I pulled away from Steven and glared at them. "There's not going to be any wedding."

"Let's not make any hasty decisions." He took my hand and pulled me toward the door. "Maybe we should go someplace and discuss the matter." He nodded toward the interested twosome glued to our backs. "Someplace a little more private."

"How do you like that?" Happy said. "We're the ones who brought them together. Now they want to sneak off someplace to discuss their wedding plans."

"Don't be silly, Happy," Lula Mae replied. "Everyone knows the wedding plans are made by the girl's mother."

I gave them "the look." The one that says, you'd better back off before you become toast.

They received the message loud and clear and hightailed it out the door faster than a couple of rabbits being chased by an irate farmer. Now to set Steven straight. "There are no wedding plans in our future. At least . . . not any time soon."

He grinned. "Are you sure about that?"

I backed up. "Pretty sure."

"Maybe you should give it a little more thought."

Before I could object, he slid an arm around my back and drew me in for another kiss.

I know how crazy it sounds, but I'm pretty sure I heard bells ringing.

Wedding bells, if I'm not mistaken.

Maybe there was a wedding in our future, after all.

ABOUT THE AUTHOR

Teresa LaRue grew up in a small town along the Mississippi Gulf Coast. She's worked as a secretary, assistant manager of an audio book store, and manager of a fashion jewelry store. She is an avid reader, gardener, and movie buff. She lives across the lake from New Orleans with her husband, two of her children, a dog named Bones, and a cat named Chloe.